A NOVEL BASED ON THE LIFE OF

MARCUS CICERO

SAVING
THE REPUBLIC

Eric D. Martin

THE **M**
MENTORIS
PROJECT

Barbera Foundation, Inc.
P.O. Box 1019
Temple City, CA 91780

Copyright © 2017 Barbera Foundation, Inc.
Cover photo: istock.com/alessandro0770
Cover design: Suzanne Turpin

More information at www.mentorisproject.org

ISBN: 978-1-947431-03-4

Library of Congress Control Number: 2017956758

The Mentoris Project is a series of novels and biographies about the lives of great Italians and Italian-Americans: men and women who have changed history through their contributions as scientists, inventors, explorers, thinkers, and creators. The Barbera Foundation sponsors this series in the hope that, like a mentor, each book will inspire the reader to discover how she or he can make a positive contribution to society.

Contents

Foreword

First and foremost, Mentor was a person. We tend to think of the word *mentor* as a noun (a mentor) or a verb (to mentor), but there is a very human dimension embedded in the term. Mentor appears in Homer's *Odyssey* as the old friend entrusted to care for Odysseus's household and his son Telemachus during the Trojan War. When years pass and Telemachus sets out to search for his missing father, the goddess Athena assumes the form of Mentor to accompany him. The human being welcomes a human form for counsel. From its very origins, becoming a mentor is a transcendent act; it carries with it something of the holy.

The Barbera Foundation's Mentoris Project sets out on an Athena-like mission: We hope the books that form this series will be an inspiration to all those who are seekers, to those of the twenty-first century who are on their own odysseys, trying to find enduring principles that will guide them to a spiritual home. The stories that comprise the series are all deeply human. These books dramatize the lives of great Italians and Italian-Americans whose stories bridge the ancient and the modern, taking many forms, just as Athena did, but always holding up a light for those living today.

Whether in novel form or traditional biography, these books plumb the individual characters of our heroes' journeys. The power of storytelling has always been to envelop the reader in a vivid and continuous dream, and to forge a link with the subject. Our goal is for that link to guide the reader home with a new inspiration.

What is a mentor? A guide, a moral compass, an inspiration. A friend who points you toward true north. We hope that the Mentoris Project will become that friend, and it will help us all transcend our daily lives with something that can only be called holy.

—Robert J. Barbera, President, Barbera Foundation
—Ken LaZebnik, Editor, The Mentoris Project

Chapter One

It was a warm day, particularly for winter. After fifty-some years in the city, Cicero could not remember a December morning hotter that this. He'd always enjoyed winters in Rome because, while sunny, they were typically crisp and refreshing. But this day was different—more like early summer than mid-winter. But for all the heat, Cicero couldn't help but notice what a beautiful day it was. A day that invited all out into the world, one in which opportunities seemed endless. Funny, he thought, that fate would present him with a day of so much promise on what would surely be his last.

The house bustled, servants and family members darting around, arms stacked with all manner of household items. On a normal day, this would not be allowed. Marcus Tullius Cicero was an introspective man and interruption worked wholly against his endeavors. Anyone who spent regular time in his home knew this and respected his need for calm. But today was not a normal day.

Cicero usually rose before his family. He liked walking the city before the citizens and merchants really got going. Walking let his mind breathe and wander. He had his best thoughts while walking. Most if not all of his written works were filled with thoughts he had, not at his desk, but while on his feet, promenading through his beloved Rome. Looking around his buzzing home on this chaotic morning, he half-considered heading out for a stroll. Surely the streets could not be as busy as his hallways. How was a man to think amidst such chaos? On a normal day, he would just not allow this. But, he thought, today is not normal.

"Father, please hurry," Tullia said.

Cicero turned to see his daughter and eldest child, Tullia, approaching, arms piled with linens and assorted valuables.

Cicero smiled. "I am," he said.

Tullia made a crooked face and continued on. Her father may be lying to her, but how was one to argue with the great Marcus Tullius Cicero, the greatest confuter of his day? Or, perhaps of any day, she thought as she went back to emptying the villa.

As Tullia moved on with her load, Cicero continued through his home. Had it always been this large? Somehow it seemed bigger today, and more beautiful too. Frescoes covered the walls and there were intricate tile patterns across the floor, with busts and statues scattered throughout. He knew all these items existed. He saw them every day. But today, he was actually *noticing* it all. It really was quite stunning. Each piece represented hours, days, months, and maybe even years of someone's life. The care and craftsmanship put into everything around him gave him pause. He hadn't enjoyed the beauty of it all nearly enough. For the first time this morning, he felt emotional.

Through the tumult of recent times Cicero had remained stoic. An uncommonly pragmatic man, he always faced problems with zeal, each quandary an opportunity to learn that which he hadn't already known. There was no place for emotion in problem solving, and fighting to preserve the Republic was just another problem he was trying to solve. What was good for the Republic was good for him. It was simple logic—the same kind of simple logic that filled his mind in most waking hours. But, he thought, maybe he had been too intent on carrying out his tasks to really appreciate the world around him. He'd been too focused on each step along the path to look up and appreciate his surroundings.

Cicero ran his fingers along the fresco of Rome stretching over the expansive atrium wall. The fresco, sprawling and crafted with intricate detail, presented the whole of the city as seen from the Palantine Hill. Amazing, he thought, that one could recreate something like this from memory. How intimidating a canvas must this wall have been! How could one work up the nerve to even *start* such an endeavor? Running his hand over the fresco and tile inlays, Cicero slowed, noticing the individual brush strokes. All big things start small and build, stroke by stroke, tile by tile.

As taken as Cicero was with the newly appreciated art of his everyday life, he began to worry. Each piece before him was crafted by a citizen of Rome and stood before him as evidence of a person's life. In all his work fighting for the Republic and its people, maybe he had failed to properly admire them and all the beauty they had created. While he fought for the whole, did he ignore the parts that made it up and made it worth fighting for in the first place?

With a wave of melancholia washing over him, Cicero felt the sudden need to get away from the madness swirling around in the house. Ducking into the hallway, he walked toward his library. Surely sanctuary could be found there. Though his staff was careful to keep a staid atmosphere in the home, they were doubly careful to ensure that no worldly bother breached the walls of the library. On an ordinary day, Cicero could enter the room and leave the rest of the world behind, but he worried that such might not be possible today. Walking into the library, Cicero paused, shocked and relieved to find the room both empty and silent. By this measure, at least, this day was mercifully ordinary.

Cicero peered around at the shelves of scrolls filling all the space but for a small outcropping occupied by his desk. Surrounding him was knowledge from as much world as he'd known to exist. He'd gathered many of the scrolls himself—writings from Greece, Egypt, and Asia. They represented not just his travels and experiences but the collective wisdom that informed the man he came to be.

There were so many scroll rolls! When did his collection grow to this prodigious size? Just like he took for granted the artistic craftsmanship all around his home, Cicero was struck that he never really stepped back and looked on his collection as a whole like this. But this is different, he thought. He may not have taken the pleasure he could have at the art all around him, but he had certainly extracted every piece of knowledge and pleasure from his scrolls. In fact, he didn't even need the scrolls anymore—numerous though they were, he knew them inside and out. Each had been read to the exhaustion of its ideas. It was a comforting thought and one that assuaged the guilt he'd felt for taking his surroundings for granted. There was too much in the world to take in everything. He may have missed some things, but he had taken in much.

Moving through the library, Cicero ran a hand along shelves, his fingers slipping along the edges of the many rolls. He

stopped as he got to his own works, again struck by their number. He stepped back. He'd never really admired the breadth of
his work because he had always been so busy working on his next
piece that he had never really stepped back to look on his work
as a body. There were so many rolls—so many words and ideas.
How had he ever had the time? He smiled as the answer came to
him: piece by piece and tile by tile.

Stepping outside, Cicero looked out over all of Rome. Perched
high upon the Palatine Hill, there wasn't a part of the city he
could not see. Behind him, two servants carried his desk.

"Over here," Cicero said, motioning the men toward him,
"where I can get the best view."

The two servants situated the desk; another set a stack of
papyrus, ink well, and quills upon it. Cicero saw the anxious
servants fidget.

"I'm sorry. You must all be in a terrible fright," Cicero said.
"Head home to your families. I release you from your service."
The servants passed confused looks between themselves. "It's
fine," Cicero said. "And I'm sorry I can no longer offer you work,
but look to the house maiden. She has payment for you." The
servants nodded and hurried away.

Cicero sat at his desk, peering out onto the great city. It felt
fresh and new, stirring feelings of his first days in the city as a
child. He had not liked Rome at first, but that changed with
time and experience. Finally feeling at peace, Cicero organized
the papyrus and dipped his quill. He began to write—

"Father," a perplexed Tullia said from the door. "What are
you doing?"

"Thought I'd get some writing done," Cicero said.

"What? No," Tullia exclaimed. "They're coming to kill you."

Cicero considered her remark, then lifted his pen. "Then I suppose I haven't time to waste."

Chapter Two

Perched at the window of his parents' apartment, a young Cicero looked out on the endless rows of buildings before him. With their building high upon a berm, the third-floor window offered a vantage point well beyond the many buildings around them. Despite that, the city sprawled and stretched beyond his perspective so even this elevated look was just a glimpse of the metropolis.

Before moving to Rome, Cicero had read everything he could about the great city. His family had only lived 60 miles from the city, but even within such close proximity to the cultural hub, the scroll rolls available were limited. Nothing like he had access to now. Ambivalent though he was about the move, Cicero couldn't help but find excitement in having access to more scrolls and writings than he could read in ten lifetimes.

In his many readings on Rome, Cicero had come across countless descriptions of the city, but in looking on it himself, he realized that none of them did it justice. How could they? The authors were trying to describe something that words struggled to illustrate. The city was massive—nearly one million people, he had read. Cicero didn't know there were that many people on Earth. Perhaps he knew in the abstract, but to fathom such a number was impossible. And why would they all want to live together?

Cicero had enjoyed living in Arpino. Having access to all the scroll rolls in the capital was great, but Arpino with its small population had a quiet, relaxed atmosphere that allowed a mind to breathe—nothing like the constant swirl of dense human occupation in Rome. Maybe they could move back to Arpino and have scrolls sent to them. That would work. It would be better. His family had moved to Rome for his education, but they could move back and he could teach himself with the scrolls from Rome. It was a good plan, but Cicero knew the answer would be the same as it always was: We're here for your schooling, so you have to go to school. Unfortunately for Cicero, school is what he liked least about Rome.

"You're not dressed," Cicero's mother, Helvia, said from the doorway.

Cicero turned from the window. "Maybe I shouldn't go," Cicero said. "You know, we can have scrolls sent to us anywhere. I can just read them and teach—"

Helvia tossed Cicero's school clothes at him. "You're going to school no matter what," she said. "Keep stalling and you'll just go without breakfast." Helvia cocked her brow and stared at Cicero a moment before leaving.

Cicero sighed and started dressing. He'd been through this enough to know that his mother always won.

Cicero wiped sweat from his forehead as he peered up at the sun overhead. It was another hot summer day; the days are always hot in Rome, Cicero thought, as he walked down an alleyway toward the thoroughfare. The problem was just too many buildings, which stifled the breeze and made the city bake in the sun. Arpino had fewer buildings and those buildings were far apart, so even on hot days, a gentle breeze could glide through. But, as annoying as the heat was, for Cicero the real problem was that there were just too many people.

During the first of his days in the city, Cicero's mother put him right out on the streets and made him walk to school. He had to learn how to get around the city some time, she said, as she booted him from the comfortable confines of their home. And learn he did. First, he learned not to walk by the brothels and drink houses. Drunks always spilled out of those places and there was no telling what a person so out of control could do. Better to go the long way around.

The long way, though it added a good deal of distance, was free of the dark, narrow alleyways that plagued the city. Rome had grown organically, with little planning, so it was a maze of pathways that all looked alike and never seemed to lead where you thought they would. Taking the long way, however, kept Cicero on wide thoroughfares big enough for shopkeepers to bring through stout oxen, yoked at the head of supply carts. Unfortunately, the long way also included a trip through the Aventine, a plebeian neighborhood.

The people of the Aventine seemed fine enough to Cicero. He liked their frank, hardworking nature; it reminded him of home. Their kids, however, scared him. They were rough and tumble and confident in the ways of the city that he was not. Plus, most of them didn't go to school, so there was little he had in common with them. On his first trips through the neighborhood, the boys—and even some of the girls—had given Cicero a hard time, but nothing more than some name-calling and jeers about being a rich boy and a dandy. Cicero tried to explain to them that he wasn't rich. His parents had some money from their farmland in Arpino, which gave them a decent middle-class life, so he could imagine how he seemed wealthy to impoverished plebeian children, but he was certainly no patrician. Such a distinction, however, was lost on the plebe kids, so Cicero learned to keep his head down and his mouth shut as he walked through their neighborhood. Even so, he wished them no ill will; he just wanted to get by them as fast as possible.

Despite having finally figured out how to navigate through the Aventine without drawing too much attention from these kids, the day Cicero discovered his current route to class was bittersweet. It had taken over a week of trial and error to discover this path through the madness of the city. The route wasn't perfect, and Cicero certainly would have preferred to avoid the plebe kids, but he was certain it was the swiftest, safest route.

The city was still intimidating, but he had made his way through it on his own and felt a little less overwhelmed by it all. It was at this moment, walking around feeling confident and proud of his ability to get around the city, that he realized he had been too overwhelmed by everything to appreciate the multidimensional aspects of walking through Rome. He had been so concerned about moving front, back, left or right that he hadn't properly factored in the difficulties that could occur at any time.

As he neared the area of the incident, Cicero remembered the awful moments as clearly as if they had just happened, and he suspected that he would for the rest of his life. He had begun the day with the confident step of a young man who knew his way, one who had been thrust into the city and who had found the optimal route to class. But as Cicero walked now, free of concern for the first time since moving to Rome, he wasn't thinking of where he was going. The sound of his foot plopping into the wet mess was the first thing that struck him. Quickly after, it was the smell, then the oozing wetness filling his sandals and washing around his feet…he had stepped in a puddle of human waste, no doubt from the dreadful practice Romans had of tossing their chamber pots out into the street. He had neglected to remember this morning ritual of the typical Roman and now his foot and leg were soiled. But in a few seconds, this would be the least of his worries.

Looking back now, Cicero recalled that he knew what was coming next. He hadn't seen the woman reach out from the third-floor apartment overhead. Nor had he heard the scrape of her chamber pot against the wood of her window well. Instead, his conclusion came as a mix of knowledge that the waste on his foot had come from above mixed with the gut-wrenching intuition that fate was about to punish his prior overconfidence.

In Arpino, people empty their chamber pots into unpopulated areas. They had land all around, so stepping outside to toss the waste off a hillside was no ordeal. Cicero knew that such was not the case in Rome, but he had not considered that someone might be on the other end of such an act. When Cicero realized what he had stepped in, he finally got around to considering how the waste got there in the first place. It took just a moment to realize the answer, but by that time it was already too late.

The contents of the chamber pot came all at once. If disgust had not overcome his ability to evaluate the situation in total, Cicero would have been amazed that nearly all the matter struck *him* alone, making its way to the ground as it dripped from his soaked robes. He threw up and cried and threw up again. But when nobody came to his aid, he turned and made his way back home, taking the short route this time. Even a drunkard wouldn't bother someone covered in the mess he was covered in.

Today, Cicero knew far more about the city and while he moved about confidently, he also knew to move with caution. Since that dreadful day, he had managed to avoid a similar fate, though he had seen many others who had not been so lucky. He learned from his mistake and vowed daily never to repeat it. However, when considering what he was marching toward at school, Cicero thought briefly that maybe being doused by a chamber pot and getting to go home might be a better fate.

Cicero gripped his hands together, hoping it might keep the boys from seeing them shake. Surrounding him stood four boys that looked a few years older, but that was just because Cicero was so small for his age. At the head of the boys stood Fabius, tall and strapping, with a lightly tanned face and dark hair over broad shoulders. The de facto leader of the group, Fabius had learned early on how to use his size to intimidate smaller boys. But for all Fabius's size, Cicero couldn't help but notice his soft, uncalloused hands. Cicero's hands were no different, but for a boy who presented himself as a physical threat, the patrician Fabius had likely done little physical labor in his life. Nonetheless, Cicero cowered before him. Fabius may have been softer than he appeared at first blush, but Cicero was still the small, weak boy he had always been.

When he was born, Cicero's parents Helvia and Tullius were told he would likely not live out the week. The doctors said they would do what they could, but he was far too small, sickly, and weak to survive. So tortured and fraught with sickness was Helvia's pregnancy that her midwife thought she would miscarry well before term. Instead, on January 3, 106 BC Marcus Tullius Cicero was born, and a week later he was still alive.

Despite a penchant for defying predictions of his death, Cicero continued to receive such prognoses throughout his early childhood. Doctors came through Arpino, did what they could for his weak immune system, and told his parents that their son would likely die before his next birthday. But birthdays kept passing and Cicero kept defying the predictions of his doctors. Nonetheless, he was sick most of the time.

As the other kids in the village grew strong and robust, Cicero remained small and weak. His mind, however, was crisp. Before his third birthday he was reading and, when well enough, he sat in on classes with the teenage students by the time he was six.

As smart as Cicero was, various maladies kept him out of school for irregular but inevitable intervals. If a sickness passed through the classroom, Cicero was sure to get it and none would have a more acute case than him. Shortly after his eighth birthday, Cicero fell gravely ill. As his condition worsened, his parents had to face the reality that this would be the time he finally succumbed to the predictions. Tullius and Helvia sat with Cicero through the night, keeping vigil for fear that they might miss the moment that would be his last. But the moment never came. Instead, Cicero awoke the next morning and each morning thereafter. He recovered from the illness and grew stronger and healthier with each day, and never again would he fall so gravely ill.

After his sickness Cicero returned to school and with his newfound vigor, his mind grew even sharper. In just his tenth year of life, no tutor in Arpino had the knowledge or ability to teach much less to keep up with young Cicero. Seeing his special abilities, Tullius and Helvia sold most of their farmland and moved to Rome to get Cicero the best instruction available.

Despite his hard-earned health, Cicero was still small for his age and, much to his chagrin, even for ages much younger than his own. In the right situation, a small eleven-year-old such as himself might be able squeak by with minimal bullying, but, as Cicero looked around at the large patrician boys that surrounded him, he knew this was not such a situation.

"You don't have the right answer now, do you, know-it-all?" Fabius barked at Cicero. As if being small and not of patrician birth were not enough to draw the scorn of the other boys, Cicero was hated in his class because he was so much smarter than everyone else. In a week he was scheduled to move up into classes with much older boys. Cicero would have been excited to get out of his current situation, but he knew that studying with even older kids was not going to make it any better. But none of that mattered, because his current bullies were already surrounding him.

"Where's the money?" one of the other boys snarled.

"I don't have any money," Cicero said.

"Then you better bring some tomorrow," Fabius said, jangling his coin purse. "I'm starting to get a little low."

"But your families have far more money than mine," Cicero said, at which Fabius smacked Cicero in the face. Cicero recoiled and the other boys laughed.

"Just bring the money or I'll hit you again," Fabius said as he and his cohorts walked off, chortling.

Cicero held his eye and sulked, as Fabius wrung out his hand, trying to hide the pain he felt from inflicting the blow.

∾

As Helvia prepared dinner, Cicero slipped in through the front door. Their apartment was spacious and well lit. It was not as nice and airy as their house in Arpino, but by non-patrician standards, it was very nice for Rome. Sneaking through, Cicero knew the loose floorboards to avoid, but his efforts were nothing compared to his mother's heightened hearing.

"Is that you, Cicero?" Helvia asked from the other room.

"Yes, Mother," Cicero responded.

"Get changed and come help with dinner," Helvia said.

"Yes, Mother," Cicero said, as he ducked not into his room, but that of his parents. Skulking through, he took even greater care not to step on a creaky board, as he moved to the ledge where his mother kept her coin purse.

Getting to the far end of the room, Cicero looked back to make sure his mother was nowhere to be seen. Satisfied she wasn't, he snatched the purse and began pilfering—

"So, you're a thief now?"

Cicero spun around, dropping the coin purse and spilling its contents across the ground, some of which rolled to the feet of his stern-faced mother.

"I was just—"

"Stealing. I saw," Helvia said. "You know, I just can't believe you would—" Helvia spied Cicero's blackening eye. "What happened?"

"Nothing. It's nothing," Cicero said, as he snatched up coins from the ground. "I was just taking the money to buy a toy."

Helvia cocked an eyebrow. "I might have believed you if you had said a scroll roll. Come here, let me look at that eye." Helvia pulled Cicero to the window, examining his eye in the light. "You got in a fight?" Helvia asked.

"No," Cicero said.

"Then explain this black eye," Helvia insisted.

Cicero hedged. "Well," he said, "I think it only counts as a fight if you fight back."

"Then why didn't you fight back?" Helvia asked.

"Because he's bigger than me," Cicero said.

Helvia considered. "And the money is for him?"

Cicero nodded, ashamed. "He said he won't beat me up if I give it to him."

"And you believe him?" Helvia pressed.

Cicero hadn't considered whether or not to believe Fabius. "I don't know. I hate it here. I want to leave. I want to go back to Arpino," Cicero said, hanging his head.

Helvia put a finger to Cicero's chin, tilting his face to look at her. "Come on," she said. "I want to show you something."

Grasping a handful of her dress in her hand, Helvia cinched the fabric up to keep it from dragging along the ground as she marched up Janiculum Hill. Cicero scurried behind, doing his best to keep up as the dust and weeds induced sporadic sneezing and coughing fits. He wanted to ask how much farther they needed to walk, but he learned long ago that if his mother thought he was complaining she'd only make the task more difficult.

Even though he wasn't enjoying the trek, Cicero valued the time with his mother. She was tough on him, but never mean. She worried about him and wanted to make sure that he grew into a strong and capable man. He knew she only ever did what was best for him, which made Cicero feel all the more guilty for not being strong.

"I think that's good," Helvia said, turning to look at Cicero. "Let's sit down."

Out of breath, Cicero happily obliged. Turning to take a seat on the hillside, Cicero paused, realizing just how high up they'd trekked, as the widest view of the city he'd ever seen stared back on him.

"What do you see?" Helvia asked.

"I see Rome," Cicero responded.

"What else?" Helvia pressed.

Cicero looked on the city. It was actually quite beautiful from this distance, even more so with the soft glow of the evening sun hanging over it. It was almost enough to make him regret his negative feelings about the place. Almost.

Cicero focused, trying to figure out what his mother wanted to hear.

"I see buildings."

"What kinds?"

"Lots of kinds."

"What do you see most of?"

Cicero considered a moment. "Homes."

"Who lives in those homes?"

"People. Romans."

"Just like you."

"I'm not a Roman."

"You may have grown up in a province and not in the city," Helvia said, "but you are a citizen of Rome, same as each and every person in this city."

"But I'm not like everyone else here," Cicero retorted.

"No," Helvia said, "and they aren't like each other. Rome isn't a place, Son. It is the sum of its people: some are smart; some are not. Some are strong; some are weak. Some were born here; some were not. But we all work together to be *Rome*. And that means something."

Cicero looked on the city again, trying to digest his mother's words.

"Do you remember when you were sick?" Helvia asked. "You couldn't get out of bed, but the doctors came to see you. They worked to heal you. *That* is Rome."

"I don't understand," Cicero said.

"I wake up every morning grateful to be Roman," Helvia said, brushing back her son's hair. "Because Rome saved your life. Rome is a republic. We have no king. The people govern themselves by electing leaders. And because of that, we all live together as one, working to make Rome great, and because of that, we have the time and resources to protect and preserve everyone. In Gaul or Germania, only the strong of body would survive. They are a separate, feuding people and because of that, they have to work harder to just survive. In Rome, the weakest of body can survive and bring value to the world in their own way."

"So, maybe I can be consul of Rome some day?" Cicero asked.

"Perhaps," Helvia said. "We moved to Rome because your mind is strong, but it needs to be with other strong minds to reach its potential. And because we, and you, owe it to Rome to give back to the republic and keep it great for all those who come after you. People who wouldn't have had a chance if not for the wisdom and resources of the Romans."

"Why are you telling me this?" Cicero asked.

"Because you need to learn to live in this world," Helvia said. "You owe it to yourself and you owe it to the republic that you fulfill your abilities, and you can't do that by running from bullies."

"But they're stronger than me," Cicero said.

"And there will always be men who are physically stronger than you," Helvia said. "But you are a man of Rome. You don't need the strongest body to be the strongest man."

Walking back, Cicero thought about his mother's words and he thought about the city. Perhaps being overwhelmed by all the people constantly swirling around caused him to be rash in his assessment of Rome. Maybe his mother was smarter in her assessment. It was the people of Rome who made Rome *Rome*. It may be difficult dealing with so many different kinds of people all in one place, but maybe that was the key to its greatness. Rome gave all manner of people a chance to add to the whole. How could any nation compete with such a wide and diverse talent pool?

Finally returning home, Cicero had dinner with his parents, but retired early to his room to read. However, as much as he wanted to read, his mind wandered, pondering the coming events at school tomorrow and how he would deal with the bullies. Realizing he'd never be able to focus enough to read it, Cicero set down his scroll and snuffed out the candle. He rolled over and settled in, ready to sleep. Instead he tossed and turned, a restless mind in a restless bed.

The next morning Cicero left early, sneaking out while his mother prepared breakfast. This meant leaving behind his lunch, but that didn't bother him much because his nerves had rendered inert any normal hunger pangs he might have had that day.

Walking to class, Cicero took his normal route. His mind was elsewhere, but he remained aware of his surroundings, careful to dodge any murky puddles as he made his way through the area where the poor plebeian boys always gave him a hard time.

Cicero took his seat in class and tried to go about his business. Perhaps, he thought, if he ignored the bullies, maybe they would forget about him too. When the first pebble struck the back of his head, Cicero knew he would not be so lucky.

The usual jeers and pestering came at Cicero from Fabius and his cohorts throughout the day. Cicero endured and did his best to pretend not to notice them. Maybe if he kept a stiff upper lip they'd lose interest and leave him alone, he thought. Class ended and Fabius approached, jangling his coin purse, and Cicero knew he would have to deal with the situation.

"Where's my money, Sissy-ro?" Fabius mocked.

"I didn't bring it," Cicero said, packing his satchel.

"What do you mean you didn't bring it?" Fabius said.

"I—I just didn't." Cicero got up and hurried for the door. Perhaps, if he just kept on, they'd leave him alone. Instead, the bullies followed.

"So, you want me to punch you then?" Fabius said, hovering over Cicero as they stepped out into the street.

"No," Cicero said walking as fast as he could.

Fabius grabbed Cicero from behind, pressing him up against a rock wall. "I told you to bring me money," Fabius said.

"But we're all Romans. We shouldn't fight like this," Cicero said.

Fabius laughed. "You're no Roman, Sissy-ro. You're a provincial. *I* am a Roman. All my friends are Romans. You are not a Roman," Fabius said, shooting his fist into Cicero's gut. Cicero lowered onto one knee, cringing in pain, as Fabius loomed over him. "You want another?"

"No, I have money at home. I can give it to you," Cicero said, crawling to his feet and starting his march home. Fabius and his friends traded nods, then followed closely behind him.

Cicero tried to talk the boys up as they walked. Perhaps, if he kept talking, they'd like him and he wouldn't need to do this. But Fabius only grew bolder in his mocking.

Through the roads and alleyways, Cicero led the boys. The farther they went, the more Cicero sensed the unease within the bigger boys. They hadn't ventured into an area like this before, he supposed. Somehow, they considered themselves more Roman than him, but they'd never spent any time with anyone other than the upper class of the city. Here he was, a weak, sickly little boy moving without concern through the plebeian area while the much larger, richer boys grew more concerned with each block.

Cicero slowed and looked to Fabius. Perhaps he could reason with them now that they had seen how confident he was ambling through the city. "Are you uncomfortable in this area? Do you not want to go further?" Cicero asked.

Fabius looked around nervously, but stiffened up, trying to hide his nerves. "I'm not scared, Sissy-ro," Fabius said, shoving Cicero to the ground.

"Very well," Cicero said, standing and dusting himself off as he headed down the next alley. Fabius and the other bullies followed but stopped short as two teenage boys stepped behind them, blocking off the entrance. Cicero continued to the other side, as two more tough boys blocked the exit. Cicero slowed, approaching Aelius, the largest of the ruffians.

"This 'em?" Aelius asked Cicero in a thick street accent.

"Yes," Cicero said. "The big one carries a coin purse."

As Fabius's jaw dropped, Cicero stepped past the big plebeian boys, ready to continue his walk home.

"Don't you want a cut of the money?" Aelius asked Cicero.

"No. You take it," Cicero said. "Maybe you can do me another favor some time."

Aelius nodded, "Yeah, all right."

As Cicero walked off, Aelius and the plebeian boys approached Fabius and his friends. Cicero heard Aelius say, "So, you like to pick on my friend, do you?" Cicero only smiled.

Once home, Cicero deposited his satchel on the table and started setting the table. Helvia approached from the kitchen. "How was your day? Better?" Helvia asked.

Cicero smiled. "Yes, I made some new friends."

Chapter Three

Cicero awoke early. The sun had yet to present itself, but he was so famished he crawled out of bed and started his day. He seemed to always be hungry these days. His mother told him it was because he was growing. He certainly hoped that she was right.

Though sixteen years old, Cicero was still smaller than boys years younger. It was not as big a deal as it used to be—he didn't get bullied like he once did, but he was embarrassed to be so much smaller than the other kids.

Over the past few months Cicero had grown another notch higher on the board his mother had used to mark his height since he was a child. In half a year he had marked three notches taller. Even so, he was still painfully skinny. It was certainly not for a lack of effort that he remained so skinny, as every time he sat down for a meal, he ate well past the point of being sated. Unfortunately, he did not always remember to sit for all his meals. More often than not, Cicero got so carried away with his studies and writings that he just forgot to be hungry. Buried deep in a thought, it was hard to pull himself away from the page, and he missed many a meal as a result.

Cicero's father, Tullius, got home late that night, so when Cicero got out of bed he took special care to move around the apartment quietly. Getting to the kitchen, he saw that his mother had left some grapes and olives for him on the wooden bench, as well as fresh dough and some coins for the baker. Cicero slipped on his sandals, grabbed the dough and quietly slipped out, munching on the grapes and olives as he did so.

After a quick wait in the bakery line, Cicero stamped the dough with his family mark and passed it to one of the bakers. It was crowded this morning, but Cicero had helped the baker a few months ago, so his dough went straight into the oven instead of waiting in the queue. Cicero had seen the one-by-one process the bakers were using to rotate out the cooked loaves and rotate in the raw dough and made some suggestions to the owner. At first, the owner laughed Cicero off. The bakery was one of five in the city owned by the same family that had been in the bakery business for centuries. How could some kid know better how to do this than them? But Cicero kept showing up and making his suggestions and finally they decided to give it a try, if just to shut him up. That first day, they served forty extra patrons in half the usual wait time. After a few more days spent working out the kinks, the results were even better.

The owners offered Cicero money and a job, but he just asked them to bank up that goodwill. One never knew when and from whom a favor could be useful. Besides, Cicero had his sights set on a career in law, not baking. And if he did well enough in law, a move into the political sphere could be in his future. That said, Cicero happily accepted the kindness of the baker in moving his dough to the front of the line.

With some time to pass as he waited, Cicero stepped outside to watch the people of the busy business district flutter about. It was still early, so many of the shopkeepers were still setting up for the day. Cicero loved this area of the city. Everyone was swirling about, working, doing business, and they were all doing it all together. It made him feel a part of a community—something larger than himself.

Poking his head back into the bakery, Cicero saw his loaf being pulled from the oven. Unfolding the cloth to wrap around the hot loaf, Cicero stepped forward but stopped short as a centurion marched into the square, flanked by half a dozen soldiers. Active soldiers within the walls of the city wasn't just rare, it was prohibited, so their presence stopped everyone in their tracks.

Cicero watched as the centurion marched into a building, leading four of his men, while the remaining soldiers stood guard at the doorway. Within seconds, the centurion exited, his men following close behind while dragging a well-heeled man with them. Cicero recognized the man because he'd seen his father talk with him, and Cicero remembered the man's futile attempts to cover his growing bald spot with some wisps of longer hair.

As the solders carried the man away, Cicero turned and darted home, leaving his bread on the counter, unclaimed.

Cicero's legs ached as he pounded up the steps to his parents' flat. He reached the third floor and threw open the door.

Helvia, reading in the corner, sat upright at upon arrival. "Oh good, you're back!" Helvia spied Cicero's empty hands. "Didn't you get the bread?"

"Where's Father?" Cicero asked.

"He's dressing. I thought you took the dough from the counter," Helvia said.

"What? I need to talk to Father," Cicero said.

Tullius entered. Though taller and with a broader build, Tullius shared his son's kind face and sharp, intelligent eyes. "What's going on?" Tullius asked, seeing Cicero's concerned gaze.

"Your friend. Uh…the man with the thinning hair…" Cicero said.

"Crispus?"

"Yes, Crispus. He was taken."

"Taken? What do you mean? "

"I don't know. I was waiting at the bakery and some soldiers—"

"Soldiers? How many?"

"Six, I think. And a centurion."

Tullius sighed deeply, and slumped into a chair.

"Is he unhurt?" Helvia asked Cicero.

"I think so. He was when they took him," Cicero responded.

"Oh dear," Helvia said. "Where did they take him?"

But Tullius had already collected his things and moved toward the door. "I know where he is," he said.

"Let me go with you," Cicero said.

"No, you go to school," Tullius responded, snatching up his coin purse.

"But I want to help," Cicero said.

"You will. Tonight," Tullius said, looking back as he hurried out the door. "I'll be back to get you."

Light flickered from a lamp's flame, sliding from building to building as Cicero followed closely behind his father. They moved quickly, navigating the narrow streets and alleyways with an accuracy that surprised Cicero. During the day Cicero could make his way through the maze of Rome just fine, but at night it was an ordeal. Signs and landmarks that marked the way during the well-lit day hours hid in the darkness at night. Nonetheless, Tullius knew just the way.

Direction wasn't the only worry for a nighttime traveler making his way through Rome. While it was certainly easy to get turned around and lost in the dark, the real danger was the people lurking in the shadows. Rome was remarkably safe during the day, but at night all manner of raiders and thieves found cover in the shadows, waiting for an unsuspecting person to pass by. Going any distance at night was always dangerous, but with no moon the night was unusually dark.

Cicero stayed close to Tullius as they made their final turn and approached a large wooden door in a patrician area of town. Tullius rapped on the door, banging out a rhythm of six knocks.

A window on the door slid open, revealing a suspicious pair of eyes. "We've already given our alms for the day. Come back in the morning," the voice from within said as its owner began to slide the window shut.

"I am Tullius Cicero."

The window now half-open, the eyes assessed first Tullius, then Cicero. "And who is he?" the voice said.

"My son," Tullius said. The eyes lingered on young Cicero a moment. Finally, the door unlatched and opened, revealing the wizened older man who had been questioning them. With a wave, the doorman motioned them forward into the estate.

The doorway, it turned out, did not even open into the house. Instead, they passed through an outdoor area of the villa, surrounded by tall, protective walls. Workers moved throughout, some tending to animals in the stables, others manicuring and cleaning the space. Cicero marveled at the amount of living space. It was enough for ten families and they hadn't even gone into the house yet.

Following the doorman into the domicile, the cacophony of a room filled with impassioned conversation fell silent as the men within turned in near unison to the newcomers. The man at the center of the fray nodded to the doorman. "This is everyone. Lock the gates. Don't even answer a knock." The doorman nodded on his way out, latching the door behind him.

The man at the center of the room stepped upon a bench. "Thank you, men, for braving the night streets. I know there is danger out there, but there is a far deeper danger infecting the whole of our republic. I believe you all know me, but if you do not, I am Luscious Cornelius Sulla. And if you indeed do not know me, ask your friends: I am a serious man. And as a serious man, I cannot stay silent."

Tullius looked to Cicero. "Stay quiet. Just watch and listen."

"Marius and his attack dog Cinna have become tyrants," Sulla continued. "A citizen of our Republic may only serve as consul for one year, then they must cede control to the next man. But Marius has used his military might to force the Senate to name him to seven consulships. At first, we stepped aside. We didn't want to make waves. We all live so well, so why jeopardize it? But power has corrupted Marius, and now, at the slightest provocation he sends his men to silence the brave vocal men among us. And those men never return."

Cicero watched, transfixed by Sulla's powerful words. These past few years Cicero had seen anger grow over Marius's refusal to relinquish power, but only now, hearing the meticulously spoken words of Sulla, did Cicero feel connected to it all. Of course intellectually Cicero was aware of the dangers of a tyrant, but there was something galvanizing about Sulla's words and the way he spoke them.

As Sulla continued, Cicero listened and watched. Sulla wasn't a large man, so in a crowd he did not automatically stand out as a leader, but his stentorian voice and stout, resolute manner gave him a rare aura of authority. Perhaps, Cicero thought, in a world such as theirs power did not have to come from physical might. Perhaps ideas and knowing how to present them was enough to lead men.

Sulla rounded out his outcry against Marius with a call to arms, seeking strong minds to help lead the strong backs of the army he had been building. Going against Marius will mean all-out war, but not the kind of war to which Rome was accustomed. There would be no foreign foes to wage war against: just two armies made up of Romans, killing each other.

It all made Cicero uneasy. Romans fighting each other could destroy everything their society was built on; the republic itself was at stake. On the walk home, in bed that night, and for many days after, Cicero's mind dwelled on the uncertain future of Rome.

In the weeks after visiting Sulla's villa, the great man's words ran constantly through Cicero's head. Having wrapped up his free-wheeling studies, Cicero's focus had moved toward becoming a lawyer, but what good was the law if the men in charge of enforcing broke it at every turn? But more than anything, Cicero hated bullies and Marius was certainly a bully.

Cicero knew his decision was an emotional one at its core, but it was a logical one too. The republic needed to be protected and, just like his mother had told him years ago, it was his duty to do his part. When Cicero told him, his father took the news well—*very well*, in fact. But Cicero knew the real problem would be telling his mother that he had enlisted in Sulla's army.

Cicero knocked food around his plate, barely eating a bite. Helvia watched with concern. In the past few weeks she had noticed that his mind was somewhere else. She was concerned, but she also knew that a young man's passage into adulthood was difficult, so she tried not to press him. Handing Cicero a plate of olives, Helvia smiled at her son. "More olives?" Helvia said. "I got your favorite green ones. You know, the fresh ones you like so much."

Cicero waved her off. "No, thank you."

"What's wrong, son?" Helvia asked.

"Nothing. I'm well," Cicero said.

Tullius, watching from the other side of the table, leaned in to say, "Tell her, son. It's time."

Cicero looked to his father, sick to his stomach.

"Tell me what?" Helvia asked.

Tullius prodded Cicero. "Go on."

Cicero gathered himself and looked to his mother. "I've joined Sulla's army," he said. "I march out tomorrow."

Helvia's jaw dropped, then her expression quickly morphed into a smile.

"You almost had me," she chuckled until she saw that Cicero had grown more sullen. "You're serious," Helvia said. "You can't do that!"

"I already have," Cicero said.

"This is a good thing," Tullius said, as Helvia's sharp eyes silenced him.

"You knew he was going to do this?" Helvia said, staring daggers at Tullius. "You encouraged this, didn't you?"

"It was my idea. I just told Father today," Cicero said.

"Well, you're not going. And that's the end of it. You're just not suited for the military," Helvia responded.

"I want this," Cicero said.

"Well, I don't want it for you," Helvia said. "I'm not letting you go and throw your life away. I just won't let you."

Cicero sat up straight. "This is about protecting the republic. And if I ever want to get into politics, I must have a military career," he said. "But more than anything, this is my chance to give back to the republic. I thought you'd be proud of me."

"I am proud of you, but this is a mistake, my dear. You're not meant for that kind of life," Helvia said.

Cicero stared back, confused by his mother's reaction to it all. "But I did it because of you—"

Helvia slapped Cicero across the face. It was instinctive and she regretted it immediately. She put her hand back to Cicero's face, both smiling and crying as she touched the red spot she just created. Finally, she couldn't take it any longer and darted away to her bedroom.

Cicero looked to his father. "I thought she'd understand," Cicero said. "She said I owe Rome for what it has given me."

Tullius nodded. "But I don't think this is what she had in mind, son." Tullius patted Cicero on the shoulder as he rose. "I'll go speak with her. You try to eat something."

As Tullius left the table, Cicero tried to eat, but just couldn't bring himself to get much down.

◝

The next morning, Cicero waited for his mother at the doorway. Bags packed, he was ready to leave. In fact, he was late, but Helvia had not come out of her room yet to see him off, so Cicero waited while Tullius talked with her.

Hearing his mother cry in the other room, Cicero finally couldn't take it anymore. In time, he knew she'd get over it, but for now, he needed to do his duty. Besides, the war would likely be over in just a few months. So, Cicero steeled himself and, despite the sound of his mother's sobs ringing in his ears, he grabbed his bags and left.

Chapter Four

The clanks of metal against metal filled the air, ringing out amidst the tapestry of grunts and screams from the soldiers in the fray. Ankle deep in the sodden mud of Raetia, Sulla's troops held tight in their phalanx, as fresh troops rotated in from the rear to spell those in the melee. Pushing forward against Marius's army, Sulla's men of Rome scattered their foes en route to winning the day.

Beyond the madness of the battle and up the overlooking hill, the leadership contingent surveyed the battlefield. At the edge of the group, Cicero looked on, trying to hide his discomfort with it all. In his years of service to Sulla's army, Cicero had seen many battles, but he could never quell the involuntary bouts of anxiety brought upon him by war.

Early on, Cicero's aptitude for strategy and politics had been recognized by Sulla's leadership circle, and he had moved up in the ranks. He had never had to enter the fray and directly lead troops because nobody ever mistook his scant build and staid demeanor for that of a soldier. Even if he had never been in the fighting, just being near it had made a deep impression on Cicero. He thought he'd have grown desensitized to it all by now, but he was still unable to separate himself from the fact that so many lives were being lost while all the leaders stood over the battlefield and watched.

As the fighting waned, a courier rushed into the leadership circle shouting, "Marius is dead! Marius is dead!"

"What's this?" Cicero said, stopping the panting man.

"Just received word from Rome. The tyrant Marius fell ill. He's dead," the soldier said.

As the courier rushed by, taking the message into the circle of higher-ups, Cicero considered the man's message. A young officer approached him from the side.

"Does this mean the war is over?" the young officer asked.

"It could. But Marius is not alone in his efforts," Cicero said, looking toward the officer. He didn't recognize him, but there was something about the young man. Tall, with bright, probing eyes, the young officer had a powerful magnetism to him. "I'm not sure we've met. Have you been with another regiment?" Cicero asked.

"Yes, sir. I was with the Fifth in Germania, but I got a transfer to be closer to the action," the young man said.

"And closer to the power," Cicero said.

"Yes, I suppose that too," the young officer said, as the two traded knowing grins, each seeing the strategic mind of the other.

"I don't believe you gave a name," Cicero said.

"Apologies, sir. I am Gaius Julius Caesar," the young officer said.

That night, the camp burst at the seams with ruckus energy. Waking that day, the soldiers were mired in a years-long civil war that most, Cicero included, had initially believed would last just a few months. Now, with one sudden announcement, the whole affair appeared to be over. Nobody liked fighting against their own, so the idea that they could drop arms and return home was welcome news.

In the officers' tent, the atmosphere was no less jubilant. The wine flowed as grown men drank freely and sang in a joyous chorus. Not all of them, however, as at the end of one of the long dining tables, Cicero sat, compiling his thoughts into a journal.

"Are you not celebrating?"

Cicero looked up to see young Julius Caesar approach. "Are we so certain it's over?" Cicero asked, looking at Caesar. Though three years Cicero's junior, Caesar's tall, broad stature made the age difference seem reversed.

"You heard the message. Marius is dead," Caesar said.

"But Marius was not the only man with a hunger for power within his camp," Cicero said, noticing Caesar had no wine in his chalice either. "Besides, I see you're not engaging in the merriment either."

Caesar smiled. "It would seem we have similar concerns."

"Get me more wine, Cicero," Catiline, a stern, joyless officer, said to Cicero, stepping rudely between Cicero and Caesar.

"Excuse me, sir," Cicero said.

"I said get me wine. That is an order from your superior officer, soldier," Catiline barked.

As Catiline stared at him, swaying on drunken, unsteady legs, Cicero knew he had no choice. "Yes, sir," Cicero said, standing to do his superior's bidding.

The entrance to the tent flipped open as Sulla's elite guards preceded him into the tent. The rowdy energy died down like when a pail of water is poured on a campfire as Sulla took the center of the room.

"It has been a long road and you have all given of yourselves so that Rome might be free of tyranny," Sulla said in his stentorian voice.

"To Sulla!" the men cheered, raising their glasses.

Sulla waved his hand, quieting the men.

"But we are not done. The master is dead, but his dog is loose. Cinna has taken control of Marius's forces, and he marches to meet us."

Silence overtook the room, as a group that thought the end was in sight now realized the fracas could go on and on.

"Set down your drinks and sit," Sulla said. "Outside, we can let the men enjoy their night. They've fought hard and don't need the bad news until tomorrow. But inside, we have planning to attend to."

With Sulla presiding, the officers surveyed the situation. Cicero, just a lowly junior officer, listened and considered but knew better than to speak up. Along with his slot low in the military hierarchy, Cicero had neither the training nor experience for his words to carry weight amongst the officer corps. Instead, he and Caesar sat and watched as Sulla laid out the dire situation.

Though not the military leader Marius was, Cinna had the loyalty of a number of Roman generals, which gave him the full force of their armies, doubling the strength he inherited from Marius. The combined troops formed a formidable army and one far larger than Sulla's current collection. Sulla had armies elsewhere in Italy and beyond, but none within a fortnight of reaching their camp.

"We should take the fight to Cinna. Use the advantage of surprise," a general projected to the room. "Cinna's forces are stronger and larger," he said, "but he is inexperienced in battle. Cinna will make mistakes, and they will allow us to carry the day."

Though Cinna was untrained, Cicero thought it would be near impossible to win against a force the size of Cinna's approaching army.

Other voices in the room begged Sulla to break camp and retreat. If they left now, they could be to Germania in a week, where they could ally with the local tribes. The tribes were ill-equipped and indisciplined, but their vast numbers alone would be enough to make a difference.

"No," Sulla said. "I will not retreat into the arms of the people Rome has warred with. I will not take up arms with our enemies. It is not right and it would be too demoralizing for the rank-and-file soldiers who are, right this minute, celebrating what they think is the end of the war."

As the lead advisors fought and yelled, Cicero watched in silence. He knew his place so he did not speak up, but the lack of original thought began to weigh on him. To Caesar's horror, Cicero stood.

"Parlay," Cicero said, getting no one's attention. Caesar nodded at him to sit down while he still could, but Cicero refused. "PARLAY!" Cicero said again, this time slamming his fist on the table. It was a bit more bombastic than Cicero had intended, but it worked in getting everyone's attention, something he immediately regretted, as stern stares from every corner of the room pierced his skin. Caesar leaned back, as if to say, "You're in this one alone, friend."

"What did you say?" Sulla asked.

"Parlay, sir. I said that we should parlay," Cicero croaked out, almost too nervous to talk.

Sulla looked at Cicero for a moment, then rolled his eyes. "No. I will not discuss terms of surrender with a tyrant." Sulla looked back to his senior advisors as their bickering began again.

Caesar's eyes grew big. "Are you crazy? Sit down!" Caesar said.

"No," Cicero said with a sternness that both surprised Caesar and caused him to retreat. Cicero steeled himself and again said to the group, "Not to surrender."

"What?" Sulla asked, growing fed up with the brashness of his junior officer.

"Take your seat, Cicero," Catiline said, then looked to Sulla. "I'm sorry, sir. Apparently some of my underlings do not know their place."

Cicero looked to Catiline, absorbing the anger from his superior, but took a breath and turned back to Sulla anyway. "Like you said, sir," Cicero said, "Cinna has a greater force, but he is new to military command. He knows that if he is to rule Rome, he must have the respect of the military, so he will force a battle no matter what. He'd not accept your surrender if you offered it."

"Then why am I to parlay with him?" Sulla scoffed.

"Because of what you don't know, sir," Cicero said.

Sulla looked on confused and more annoyed by the second. Cicero steeled himself, in too deep to turn back now.

"Cinna is new to military command," Cicero said, "so we don't know what we don't know about him yet. He's a total unknown, but if we parlay with him, we can go and see what he's doing wrong. See what he's doing right. We can gather more information in a ride through his camp to a parlay than a hundred spies could get us in a year. It's the smart move, sir."

Finished, Cicero sat down awkwardly, as Catiline stared coldly at him. Actually, *everyone* was staring at Cicero.

Finally, Sulla leaned in toward the table. "How is it that one runt of a junior officer gives me better counsel than the entirety of my supposedly august and wise officer corps?" Nobody spoke up. "Yes," Sulla continued, "probably best for you all to be silent at this moment. Have you anything else to add to your plan?"

"Cicero, sir. And just that we should insist that the meeting be in four days," Cicero said.

"And why is that? Seems to me that we'd want more time to prepare," Sulla said.

"Yes, sir, time would be helpful," Cicero said, "but Cinna is a proud man, and he is no doubt anxious to prove his mettle. That's why he's going to accept the parlay in the first place. He wants to face a great man like you and show that he is in charge."

"And how does that benefit us?" Sulla asked.

"By any reasonable measure, Cinna's army is a six-day march from here," Cicero said. "But this is an exceptionally proud man, and he is so determined to be the next great man of Rome that if you set a meeting in four days, his ego will never let him admit that it's too soon."

"So what? You think we're going to get the upper hand by embarrassing him by setting a deadline he can't meet? Absurd," Catiline scoffed.

Seeing Sulla's patience wane, Cicero pressed on. "It's more than that," Cicero said. "Marius was a celebrated general and his men trusted him, but they're fighting for Cinna now and they don't know him. Cinna has to prove himself."

"He has to prove himself to his own soldiers?" Catiline said. "I think we've heard enough from you—"

"Let him speak, Catiline," Sulla said, then looked to Cicero. "Continue, Mr. Cicero."

"Thank you, sir," Cicero said, gathering his thoughts. "Perhaps we can negotiate with Cinna and perhaps not, but I bet he'll march his men hard to get here in time to have those discussions, because he doesn't want to seem weak to us or them. But to do that march in four days means keeping his troops moving day and night. And if it turns out that there's no path but to fight, it would be an advantage to fight tired men."

As Sulla mulled over these words, Cicero took a breath and sat down again. Finally, Sulla nodded and looked to his senior officers. "Well, you've heard the plan. Make the preparations necessary." Sulla looked to Catiline. "And Catiline, please don't hide talent like Mr. Cicero from me again."

Catiline forced a fake smile. "Of course not, sir," Catiline said, scowling across the table at Cicero.

Too relieved to notice Catiline's anger, Cicero sighed. Caesar gave Cicero a nod as the room cleared. "Remind me never to tell you not to speak up," Caesar told him on his way out.

As Cicero got up to follow Caesar, Sulla motioned to him. "Oh, Mr. Cicero, thank you for your wisdom."

"Of course, sir," Cicero said. "I just wanted to—"

"But if you feel the need to speak again," Sulla said, quieting Cicero, "look to your superior officer, lest you desire losing your head for insubordination."

Cicero nodded and quickly gathered his things.

"And look to my hand servant before you go," Sulla said. "If you're going to come with me to the parlay, I won't have a senior officer in such rags."

Cicero nodded, realizing he had just received a promotion. "Yes, sir, thank you, sir," Cicero said, as he hurried from the tent.

≈

Just as Cicero predicted, Cinna took the bait, accepting the invitation to parlay with Sulla. What Cicero did not predict was that Cinna wouldn't just agree to meeting in four days, he would cut it down to three days. It certainly elevated Cicero in the eyes of Sulla, but it also heaped pressure on him to continue advising Sulla with such results.

In the days leading up to the parlay, the camp swirled with activity. The rank-and-file soldiers were taken aback that the war was not only *not* over, but that it was to continue in just a few days and against a much larger force. Nonetheless, the troops rallied for the great Sulla and swore to fight to the death if need be. Cicero hoped it would not come to that.

Cicero, now in Sulla's inner circle, mostly just sat through the meetings, watching experienced military men plan for battle. Even if Cinna's men were exhausted from the march, the disparity in numbers made it very difficult to see how Sulla's forces could possibly win. On the bright side, Cinna's march would be so long and arduous that they would have no time or energy to organize a proper camp. Without an organized system of tents, latrines, and food preparation, the army would be discombobulated and vulnerable.

Now, with everything prepared on Sulla's end, the parlay party marched to Cinna's camp. Cicero, clad in an extravagant senior officer uniform, marched with Sulla. As they set out, Cicero was content to trot along in the back, but Sulla insisted he stay by his side at the front of the parade.

As the party reached the outskirts of Cinna's camp, Cicero's stomach dropped. Not only was it not chaos, it was just as organized as their own camp and nearly twice as large!

"They don't exactly look as ill-prepared as you thought they would, do they?" Sulla said, as Cicero began to fear he had set them all up for certain death. "Well," Sulla continued, "let's head in and hope all is not as well as it appears."

Sulla's calm in seeing the organized camp gave Cicero some confidence, but as they marched in, Cicero fretted to see that it was in even better shape that it appeared. Tents were still being erected, but there were latrines, food lines, fires, and even a watering trough for the horses. How could they possibly have done all this in an afternoon?

Reaching Cinna's tent, Sulla hopped from his horse and led his delegation in. Before entering, however, he looked to Cicero, cracking a mischievous smile. Cicero was taken aback. What could Sulla possibly be happy about when Cicero had clearly led them to near-certain death?

Entering the tent, Cicero stood to the back as Sulla and Cinna shared a stilted handshake.

"The great Sulla," Cinna said, smugly. "I could hardly believe it when I got word that you wished to parlay with me."

"Yes, well, we are both men of Rome. If we can avoid bloodshed, then we must," Sulla said.

"Oh, I have no intention of avoiding bloodshed. In fact, I would not accept your surrender even if you offered it without terms," Cinna boasted.

"Then it is good that I am not seeking terms," Sulla said.

"Then, I shall see you on the battlefield tomorrow?" Cinna asked.

"You shall see me this afternoon," Sulla said tartly.

"No, tomorrow at first light we march out to your battlefield." Cinna countered.

"Then, I guess we will just have to march over here to you," Sulla said.

Cinna sat back. He had not expected this. He laughed to himself.

"Today it is," Cinna said, putting his hand out. Sulla stood up too, but turned away, leaving Cinna's hand outstretched and unmet. Cinna fumed as Sulla led Cicero and the rest of the delegation from the tent.

Getting on their horses, Cicero rode up to Sulla. Cicero wanted badly to ask Sulla about his intention back in the tent, but he knew better to say anything, so he just trotted along beside him.

"You have something to say, Mr. Cicero?" Sulla said.

"Just…why give up all our advantages on our battlefield? You see how prepared they are. Even if they are tired, their numbers and preparation are enough," Cicero said.

"You're right, they may be fatigued, but that won't be enough," Sulla said.

"Then why push it like this?" Cicero asked.

"Look at these men. He marched them day and night to get here, then forced them to make camp without rest," Sulla said. "Sure, they may not be tired enough to let us win a victory, but they're angry enough to not make us fight at all!"

Cicero looked around at the downtrodden men, working their fingers to the bone. Indeed, they looked tired, but *anger* was writ large on their faces, not fatigue.

Sulla pulled the reins tight on his steed, stopping it and their procession in the middle of the encampment a few hundred yards from Cinna's tent.

"Gentlemen of Rome," Sulla called out to the opposing soldiers. "You honor me with your opposition, for there is no greater adversary for a Roman than a Roman. May we all fight and die with honor in today's battle."

Sulla kicked his horse into a gallop and led his team from the camp. Cicero hurried to follow. He was not comfortable with the speed but was too taken by Sulla's actions to not inquire about them.

"Cinna doesn't realize he's already asked too much of these men," Sulla said, basking youthfully in the moment. "If they had a full night's sleep tonight, it would be a different story, but if they are told they must meet us on the battlefield today, I suspect most will refuse the call. And Cinna is too much of a coward to step onto the field with half an army. If victory isn't assured, he will not be fighting at all, and we will be accepting his sword without a drop of blood."

Sulla kicked at his steed and darted ahead far faster than Cicero could so he sat back and marveled at the great man's reading of the situation, then rode off with zeal toward the camp.

With the soldiers assembling in marching formation in the center of camp, Cicero stood to the side, trying to clasp on his armor with shaking hands. Caesar, seeing his friend struggle, walked over to help.

"Thought you said we weren't going to have to fight. What's there to be nervous about?" Caesar asked.

"I said Sulla thinks we won't have to fight. Fate could see that we do, and I am a coward," Cicero said, as Caesar hooked the final latch on the armor.

"Bravery is the overcoming of fear, not the absence of it. You'd be a fool not to be afraid before battle," Caesar said.

"Then why aren't your hands shaking?" Cicero asked.

"Because I'm a fool," Caesar said with his golden smile.

Cicero laughed, forgetting about the battle for a moment. Just then, a group of horsemen crested the hill. At first, Cicero and the soldiers braced themselves, expecting more to crest the hill, but when only a dozen rode toward them, they relaxed.

Gaining speed, the horsemen approached the camp, and it became clear the leader was carrying something. As he trotted through the lines of soldiers, the macabre object became clear: a human head.

As Sulla exited his tent, the lead horseman slowed and tossed the head before him. Staring on the twisted face of the severed head, Cicero knew immediately it used to belong to Cinna. Sulla looked on his former foe a moment, then turned to the rider.

"Where did you get this?" Sulla asked.

"We are the officers of Marius's army. Cinna was never our leader," the lead officer said.

Sulla nodded sullenly, then looked to his second in command.

"Tell the men to break down their gear and relax. There will be no battle today," Sulla said, then motioned to Cinna's officers. "And prepare these men for execution."

Sulla's guards grabbed the horsemen pulling them from their mounts, despite their shocked pleas for mercy.

Sulla motioned for Cicero as he turned and headed into his tent so Cicero hurried in after him. As Sulla took a seat, staring off in contemplative repose, Cicero approached.

"You did well, young man. If not for your advice, many men would have lost their lives," Sulla said.

"But I am not the one who killed Cinna," Cicero said.

"And that is why you are still alive," Sulla responded. "Do you disagree with me for ordering those men dead?"

"No, sir. Just wondering why. They killed a tyrant. They prevented the battle," Cicero said.

"They killed their general. A man forfeits his life with such an action," Sulla said. "Honor dictates it." Sulla pulled his sword from its scabbard and marched from the tent, leaving Cicero behind.

Chapter Five

The days following Cinna's death were lively and jubilant. Although Cinna's men were uneasy at first, as the armies combined their mood relaxed. Of course, it did not hurt that Cinna's well-stocked supply train had wagons loaded with wine and fresh food.

The end of any war is worth a soldier's celebration, but the end of a civil war that saw so many Romans fall under the swords of their countrymen was especially sweet. Though not much of a drinker, even Cicero indulged in a few glasses of wine as he celebrated with Sulla and the officers. For two days the festivities rolled on. Some people would fall off, retiring to their quarters for a slumber, but the celebration never ceased as there were always people up and imbibing—a little too loudly for those trying to get some sleep, Cicero thought.

As the days passed, however, the festivities waned and murmurs of uncertainty grew. Soldiers were once again given orders to get work done around the encampment, but there had yet to be an order to break camp. The rank and file soldiers were restless, not knowing why they had yet to break camp and march home. With Marius and now Cinna dead, what need was there for an army?

As Cicero gave out orders to his troops on the third morning after the end of hostilities, one of Sulla's personal guards came to him.

"Lieutenant Cicero, General Sulla would like to see you," Sulla's guard said, immediately turning around and marching back.

Finally, Cicero thought, they will be getting their orders to break camp, disband the forces, and return to their homes.

Making his way to Sulla's tent, Cicero's thoughts turned to home. It had been years since he'd last seen his parents. They traded letters at first, but as the army moved further from Rome, correspondence became impossible. Cicero missed home and missed his parents, especially his mother. Missing one's mother wasn't exactly a common topic of conversation among soldiers, so Cicero mostly had to endure his loneliness in silence.

Before leaving Rome, Cicero had studied law. He was young, but he was prepared and ready to start practicing nonetheless. The goal was to work as a lawyer to establish himself and become better known by the public, then move into politics. With no lineage or wealth to put him on the path toward the *cursus honorum*, the hierarchy of Roman political leadership, the path into politics was a difficult one. Cicero hoped that with some hard work and dedication to the law, his knowledge and abilities would translate into success as a lawyer and perhaps earn him enough public repute to get onto the political playing field. It was a good plan, but it was thrust aside when Cicero felt compelled to enter Sulla's service.

Though Cicero had diverged from his intended path, military experience was helpful as an entry into politics, so in the end his service could be a boon, especially now that he was a part of Sulla's leadership circle. Nonetheless, politics was a way off, so Cicero's mind necessarily wandered to the possibilities of practicing law. It was often joked that suing each other is the favorite pastime of Romans, so he expected that work would be plentiful. He hoped to find a niche to specialize in, make some good money, start a family, and begin meeting the people necessary to build a political career. If he played his cards right, Cicero could be able to get into government as a tribune and maybe even work up to adile. It was a lofty dream and probably a bit silly given his humble lineage, but matching a stellar legal career with his military service, Cicero could get there over a lifetime.

As he approached Sulla's tent, Cicero neatened his uniform and marched past the stern and imposing guards who made him nervous each time he passed them; this time was no different. Entering the tent, Cicero expected to see a room full of officers and hoped not to be the last one to enter. The summons only just came to him, so he had an excuse, but it was never good to be the person everyone is waiting for. Cicero walked into the tent to find Sulla seated at his desk alone. Cicero wasn't the last one to the meeting, so his worries faded, but they were quickly replaced by his skittishness about visiting the great man all alone.

"Ah, Cicero. Please, take a seat," Sulla said with a welcoming arm extended.

"I'm sorry, sir. Am I too early?" Cicero asked.

"You are right on time," Sulla said. "How are your men?"

"Good, sir. They were getting restless, but I've kept them working, so all is well. Will we be breaking camp soon?" Cicero asked.

Sulla stood up and folded the map on his desk over on itself to obscure it. As Sulla did so, Cicero was just able to make out what appeared to be the edge of Rome.

"I wanted to thank you again for your great work," Sulla said. "You have a strong mind for strategy."

"Thank you, sir," Cicero said. "I'm happy to be of service. To you and to the republic."

"I'm glad you said that," Sulla said, "because I am conscripting you into more service."

Cicero's stomach sank. He had been foolish to let his mind wander to thoughts of home and a career. Surely they'd be off to battle the tribes of Germania or an uprising in Gaul. Home, he feared, would be many years off. Nonetheless, Cicero put on a brave face.

"I am happy to do my duty, sir," Cicero said.

Sulla cocked his head. "You seem…disappointed, young man."

"No, sir. I'm sorry, sir. Just surprised," Cicero said.

"No, you were thinking of home," Sulla said.

Cicero hung his head, caught. "Yes, sir," he said. "But I am ready to serve in whatever capacity you need."

"Good," Sulla smiled, "because Rome needs an new quaestor."

"Excuse me, sir?" he said, sitting up, at once shocked and confused.

"Are you not interested?" Sulla asked, needling Cicero.

"No, sir, of course I am. It's more than I thought I'd ever achieve," Cicero said.

Cicero shrugged. "But…I'm not qualified," he said. "I haven't worked in law or served in the Senate. Nobody knows me."

"Then, I suppose, it is a good thing I secured you the support necessary to get you a seat in the Senate. You can serve there until you meet the age requirements to begin the cursus honorum as a quaestor." Sulla said.

Cicero was stunned. Only members of the elite could begin the cursus honorum at such a young age. "Sir," he said, "I don't know what to say."

"Well, I hope that changes, because you're going to need to learn how to articulate your thoughts to the Senate," Sulla said. "You have a great mind, and I will need great minds to bring Rome back to its former glory."

"Yes, sir," Cicero said.

"Now go tend to your men. We have much time to talk about this later," Sulla said.

Cicero obliged and headed to his men. As he walked, his mind wandered. Never had he imagined that such a thing could be possible. Senator Cicero, he thought to himself. It had a nice ring to it.

Cicero sat at the desk in his tent, reading over a Greek philosophical text he had bartered off a trading caravan. His men had completed their work for the day, so he gave them the rest of daylight off. He would have liked to give them another task, but there simply wasn't much to do while they sat and waited in camp.

"I heard you were called to speak with Sulla."

Cicero looked up from his scroll to see Caesar entering.

"I was," Cicero said.

"And that's all you're going to give me?" Caesar pressed. "Are we moving on? Are we breaking up the army?"

"I don't know," Cicero said.

"Don't know or can't tell," Caesar asked.

"Don't know," Cicero said.

"Then why did he call you to his tent?" Caesar asked.

Cicero hedged, not sure he should say anything. Finally, he relented. "He wants to back me politically," Cicero said.

Caesar paused, not knowing what to say. Certainly this was not what he expected to hear. "Why?" Caesar finally asked.

Cicero laughed. "Why? Am I of so little value that this is such a shock?"

"No, I'm just surprised is all. It's just…this is no small thing for Sulla to do," Caesar said.

Cicero could tell Caesar was putting on a brave face. Caesar was ambitious and surely wished to be the one to have the ear of the great Sulla. And for good reason—it was an incredible opportunity. Nonetheless, Cicero knew not to celebrate openly so as to not alienate his friend.

"I just got lucky," Cicero said, in an attempt at modesty.

"No, you were smart to speak up when and how you did. You deserve this," Caesar said. "Now you just need to worry about what he wants in return."

"What do you mean? He did this because I advised him on Cinna," Cicero said, confused.

"A man like Sulla did not get to where he is by *giving* anyone anything," Caesar said. "It is always a trade."

Cicero's stomach sank. Caesar was right. Before Cicero could respond, one of his men entered the tent.

"Sir, General Sulla is summoning all officers to the leadership tent," the soldier said, as Caesar looked toward Cicero.

"Aha! And now we find out the price," Caesar said with a flourish.

≈

The last of the officer corps filed in as the leadership tent filled to capacity. Within its linen walls stood every officer serving under Sulla. Most stood around the senior leadership table in the center of the room. Space at the table was limited to the select few in Sulla's closest confidence, so while Cicero was shown to his seat, Caesar had to hang back with the rest of the lesser officers.

What started as murmurs and side conversations soon turned to a din of chatter, as everyone verbalized their thoughts and predictions about what was to be announced. Were they heading north to quell a rebellion in a province or would the army be disbanded now that the civil war was concluded? Suddenly, all talking ceased in an instant as the tent flaps opened and Sulla walked in with his pack of personal guards. Catiline, off sulking with two other officers in a corner, hurried to take a seat at the table. He scowled to see Cicero seated next to him.

Sulla marched through, shaking hands with his men and accepting their congratulations as he made his way to the head of the table. Cicero saw Caesar leading the charge of men clamoring to praise the general. Indeed, Caesar was an ambitious man.

Finally, Sulla made his way through the crowd and took his seat at the head of the table. The room grew quiet again, anticipating Sulla's words. Finally, he raised his arms and boomed, "We have won!"

The men cheered, but Sulla raised a hand to quiet them.

"But we have only won a battle. The war rages on," Sulla said, as the men looked on, not sure of his meaning. "I'm sure you've all been wondering why we've yet to disband the army and return home. Is there an uprising that must be put down? Is there another conflict elsewhere that we must attend to? Will we be traveling to face another army of insurrectionists? Marius and Cinna have perished, and now their army is ours and there is no other army to face us…but their disease runs rampant in the veins of Rome still. And until that disease is snuffed out, we must continue our battle."

Cicero and Caesar traded concerned, confused looks.

"So, my brothers-in-arms," Sulla continued, "rouse your troops, break down our camp, and march with me to cleanse our city of all those who supported the tyrants and all those who benefitted from their unjust, illegal rule. Tomorrow, we march to Rome."

The officers cheered. Caesar played the part and followed suit, but Cicero did not.

"But the work won't be completed merely by marching on the city," Sulla said. "Throughout the government and into the Senate, we have many enemies. Marius and Cinna have filled the halls with their lackeys, and I need the help of you all to purge them from their positions. Each of you will have a place in my administration, but I need your oath of fidelity. You must be loyal to me and only me. Now, are you ready to march to greatness? Are you ready to take back our republic? Are you ready to march on Rome?"

The room erupted in overwhelming applause, as Cicero alone kept silent composure, something Catiline noted as their eyes met. But in the heat of the moment, Catiline chose not call out Cicero's lack of support, but instead to march through the boisterous crowd in lock step with Sulla as he led his officers out into the camp to inform the soldiers.

Cicero waited at the table, then Caesar, at the back of the crowd, stopped beside him.

"Well, I guess we know what he wants now," Caesar said, marching out with the rest of the mob.

∾

Cicero watched his men as they broke down the tents in preparation for disembarkation. Cicero could never support marching on Rome and using the threat of an army to purge Sulla's rivals, but he also wasn't ready to refuse his general's orders either, so Cicero had ordered his men to do the necessary work while he stepped back to think about the quandary he was in. Cicero ruminated, trying to find a way to justify following orders, but he simply could not get the idea of such a great crime against the republic out of his head.

Rome was a republic built on ideals. The people elected their officials, and those officials represented the people in the government. Political office was not taken, it was granted by the citizens. To do otherwise was an affront to the republic and was bad enough, but to also march an army toward Rome, cross the Rubicon, and enter the city to seize power? That was a coup and it was a threat to the very republic itself. Rome had no king and to ensure that no citizen used force to take dominion over it, no army was allowed to enter the city. It was a matter of honor, integrity, and the rule of law. And more than that, it was the basis for the idea of Rome itself. So Cicero may have given his men their orders from Sulla so as to protect them and let them make their own choice in the matter, but Cicero would not and could not follow those orders himself.

So as his men broke camp, Cicero dressed in his tent, strapping on all the flourishes of his dress uniform to prepare himself to confront Sulla in the most respectful manner possible. Cicero would speak his mind, refuse Sulla's orders, and accept his punishment. This would likely be his last act, as Sulla would certainly kill him for insubordination. Cicero was frightened by the prospect, but it was better to retain his morals and voice his support for the republic than to give in and be a part of its fall.

So with his uniform pressed, Cicero left his tent and marched to Sulla, ready to meet his fate.

The guards ushered Cicero into Sulla's command tent, motioning him to a seat as Sulla talked with two of his generals beyond. Cicero sat and took a deep breath, his hands shaking in his lap. He tried to calm himself, but his hands knew the fate awaiting him.

Finally, Sulla waved off the two generals. "Later. We can deal with this later," he said, turning to walk toward Cicero.

As Sulla approached, Cicero tried to hide his shaking hands.

"I was twelve when my father took me to my first battle. It was supposed to be a rout, so it didn't seem like such an event," Sulla said. "But it's never an event until it becomes an event.

"Instead, the Gauls routed our army. They lost far more men, but they also had far more men to lose—enough that they could absorb the losses and keep going. The left flank folded, and soon the leadership party was fighting for its life. My father put me behind him and tried to protect me, but I could tell he already knew we were going to die. Then the rains came. I don't know if those particular Gauls just hate rain or felt they had killed enough that day, but they turned and went back to their camp. And we survived.

"I was a kid, but I had just seen more battle than any highborn officer in that army. But as I got older my hands would shake before every battle. Nothing I could do. I knew the horror that was coming to the battlefield and my body reacted accordingly. I was made fun of by men who had never and would never see death first hand. At the start I was angry, embarrassed. Then, I realized that fear is the intelligent response. If you're not afraid of losing your life, then you're not going to do much to protect it. So, I guess what I am saying is, what are you going to do to protect your life right now?"

"Nothing, sir," Cicero said.

"Then I can see why you are so nervous," Sulla said. "You do not support me marching on Rome."

"I do not, sir," Cicero said. "I am here to accept my punishment. I cannot and will not work to undermine the republic."

"I'm not trying to undermine the republic, Cicero. I am trying to save it," Sulla said.

"You can't save the republic by taking power by force. Power is given by the people, not taken," Cicero said.

Sulla nodded, losing patience. "I'm not going to be lectured to by some irrelevant coward who I just rewarded," Sulla barked.

"I meant no disrespect, sir," Cicero said. "You are a great man by any measure. And you have done an incredible service to the republic by removing tyrants like Marius and Cinna."

"Then why are you against me?" Sulla asked.

"I'm not against you, sir," Cicero said. "I am for the republic."

"The republic is broken," Sulla said. "It is filled with Marius's power-hungry minions, and the Senate is mired in its own ego. Nothing gets done unless someone can make political hay out of it and move their way up the political ladder. It needs reform."

"Then go and make your case to the people," Cicero said. "Convince the Senate to elect you consul."

"They are corrupted beyond repair," Sulla said. "The only way to convince them is to march on Rome and take power. Then I can change the system and return the republic to glory." Sulla paused, seeing that none of this was swaying Cicero. "But you disagree. There is no way to convince you, is there?"

"Respectfully, sir, there is not," Cicero said. "Marching on Rome is a precedent I cannot be party to."

Sulla considered a moment. "You know," he said, "I don't need you to do any of this. I could have killed you just as talk to you. Nothing would change."

Cicero gulped. "Yes, sir."

Sulla shook his head. "Pack your things and go."

"Excuse me, sir?" Cicero asked.

"You heard me," Sulla said. "Pack your things and leave. Wait until dark, then make your way out of camp."

"Sir, I wasn't trying to—"

"I like you, Cicero, I do," Sulla said. "I respect your honor. That's why I'm allowing you to survive this insubordination. But don't try to reason with me right now. You can leave with your head or speak your mind and lose it."

"Yes, sir," Cicero said, heading for the door.

"Good luck to you, Cicero," Sulla said.

Despite night having fallen, the soldiers continued working, motivated to break camp with anticipation of their march on Rome in the coming weeks. While his soldiers labored outside, Cicero hurried around his tent, gathering what few things he could carry on his back. With scrolls not making it in the pack, Cicero piled them on his desk next to a note instructing his men to give them to Sulla. Perhaps it was a step too bold to offer a would-be tyrant scrolls on law, but Cicero thought it was a gesture Sulla would appreciate. Sliding on his pack, Cicero extinguished his lamp and headed outside.

Beyond the flickers of the fire at the center of their camp, Cicero's men went about their duties, too entrenched in their work to notice as he slipped away.

Moving furtively along the dark pockets of the encampment, Cicero made his way toward the boundary and the dark night beyond. Approaching the edge, Cicero moved wide to avoid the light of a well-fueled fire.

Fluttering tent flaps startled Cicero, as he paused to see a figure stepping out. The figure turned to him and the two met eyes. It was Caesar. For a moment, the two men looked at each other in silence, and Caesar noticed Cicero's pack. Finally, Caesar nodded; Cicero did the same, then turned into the darkness to start his long walk home.

Chapter Six

Walking along the cobblestone road, Cicero took care to angle his right foot, stepping with its side rather than heel. He'd been doing this for two days now, because a blister on the other side had become too painful to allow him to walk any other way.

Since leaving Sulla's camp Cicero had spent the majority of each day on his feet. For some men such would not have been so out of the ordinary, but Cicero was used to time spent in repose, reading, writing, or contemplating. He enjoyed fresh air and exercise for the most part, but as the days passed, the constant activity was steadily wearing on his unconditioned body. With his feet blistered and his joints aching, he simply wished to be back in Rome.

Walking 20-odd miles a day had taken a toll on Cicero, but it was the lack of food that had really weakened him. Leaving camp in such a hurry, he was only able to pack the few provisions he had around his tent, which, when rationed out into barely reasonable servings, did not quite last him a week.

At the outset Cicero had estimated the trek to be over 200 miles, as the crow flies. Unfortunately, Cicero was no crow, so he had likely tacked on far more distance by following the snaking road around hills and rivers. How many, he was not certain, but he figured it was a good bet that he had covered over 300 miles.

Throughout his journey, Cicero passed countless milestones. Early on, the markers gave him some idea of the distance traveled, but soon the traditional milestones disappeared and were replaced with columns erected in honor of Marius. Cicero would have thought it humorous that a useful tool had been replaced by a pure vanity, but not knowing the distance left to travel was far too annoying to allow for much humor at all.

Going off-road was an option, but Cicero didn't think it best. Roadway robbers were always a concern, but Roman roads were commonly travelled and protected by soldiers. The same could not be said for the countryside, so it was safer to stick to the beaten path. Getting lost was a concern too. He might be able to shave distance from his journey by journeying off-road, but there was no guarantee that the road would turn as he expected it to. While the axiom was hyperbolic, in this area indeed all roads did lead to Rome. If he could just keep going, eventually this one would get him there. But could he keep going?

After running out of provisions, Cicero was able to purchase some food from sporadic travelers passing through. More than a few times, he considered paying for a ride on an oxen cart to get some rest, but his coin purse was growing light, so feeding himself was the more immediate concern. Like he had with the supplies he had brought from camp, Cicero metered out his purchases. As careful as he was, though, his purse was nearly empty and he was starting to get thinner. His cheeks were hollow and his shoulders, though never broad and strong, now felt stringy and weak. On the plus side, Cicero told himself, at least his decreased girth meant he had far less weight to carry as he walked.

The thought made him chuckle, but it was cold comfort to his rumbling stomach.

Despite his hunger, Cicero's mind ruminated on his future. Since childhood, Cicero had dreamed of the cursus honorum. The course of leadership within the republic had evolved over time, but in the generations prior to Cicero it had hardened into a direct path. There were offshoot offices that diverged from the course, and they were all important positions that helped organize and govern the republic, but Cicero's ultimate dream had always been to reach the highest position: consul.

To reach consul, one had to first serve as quaestor. Charged with handling the monetary interests of the republic, a quaestor could work in Rome or in a province as the second in command to the regional governor. With just twenty quaestors at a time, the position was highly sought after and difficult to attain. Success as a quaestor could lead to a step up to the ladder to praetor. Praetors exercised high levels of power in the republic leadership structure, including presiding over criminal trials and even leading military legions in the absence of a consul. But while there were twenty quaestor positions, only about six to eight praetors served at a time. The higher up the ladder, the fewer positions were available.

The final rung of the cursus honorum was consul. Consul sat at the top of the hierarchy and exercised a high amount of authority, but the position could be held for only a single year. But for all the brevity of the term, serving as consul was the pinnacle of honor in Roman leadership and the most important and powerful office. Consuls could veto any Senate vote and exercise a variety of executive powers, but the authority of the office was kept in check by limiting each office holder to just one year. That is, until Gaius Marius took power and forced his way into being elected consul seven times. His abuse of power disgusted Cicero and drove him into military service to help aid the republic. It was a pipe dream for someone without a patrician lineage and familial wealth, but Cicero hoped to work his way up to the consulship the right way and use his time there to make sure nobody else could abuse the office as Marius had done. But now that Cicero had left his post in the army and drawn the ire of Rome's greatest man, Sulla, any thought of his climbing the ladder of the cursus honorum was a fool's dream.

Approaching a rolling hill, Cicero slowed. The road typically went around mounds of this size, so he was surprised to be faced with such a trek. He was also tired and hungry. Down to the last of his money, Cicero had held off from eating and now felt the growing effects of a two-day fast, so he'd have to buy food from the next traveler.

Cicero peered up at the hill, considering stepping off the road and waiting to buy some food from the next traveler he encountered. In the meantime, he could find some shade and take a nap. But then he thought about how hard it would be to work up the motivation to climb the hill after eating and, presumably, napping. The way he felt now, if he gave in to slumber, he'd sleep right until tomorrow. It was not the most desirable option, but it was better to crest the hill now and wait for a traveler up at the top. Once he ate, it would be much easier to convince himself to keep walking if he was only looking at going downhill.

So Cicero put one foot in front of the other and marched ahead. He felt fine at first, just moving forward, trying not to think about the effort. Soon, however, his fatigue grew. Cicero's stomach growled and his head ached more with each step. He wanted nothing more than to stop and rest, but Cicero kept his eyes on the top and pressed forward.

Giving every last ounce of energy he had to the task, Cicero crested the hill, exhausted. But he did not stop like he had planned. He didn't even slow down. Instead, he hurried forward, when suddenly his hunger pangs and his splitting headache disappeared, as the simple vista he discovered at the peak cured his woes: *Rome!* Cicero moved through the city with a bounce in his step. Soon he'd be home, reunited with his parents after years apart. He would leave behind the lumpy ground in favor of a proper bed and finally get some decent sleep. And there would be food—much of it. But, as good as feasting sounded, it was simply being back in Rome that was the source of the joyous energy that Cicero felt pulsing through him. This was home and it felt good to be home.

Through roads and alleyways, Cicero made his way to his parents' home. With nary a wrong turn in the maze of stone and structures, Cicero surprised himself with his ability to navigate. He had not lost his sense of the city.

Getting to the building, Cicero hurried up the steps toward the third-floor apartment. With each step, his mind wandered. How would they react to seeing him out of the blue like this? Had they received any of his letters? What would his mother make him to eat? Surely after the hugs and merriment, his mother would be aghast at his skeletal appearance and insist he sit for a meal immediately. Even if there was nothing but bread and olives in the house, he was hungry enough that such would leave him completely sated. The hunger pangs, once quelled, returned as he dwelled on food. But that was fine, he thought, because he was almost there.

Getting to the top of the stairs, Cicero rapped on the door, opting to open it instead of waiting for an answer.

"Hello?" Cicero said. "Mother? Father? Is anyone here?"

Cicero set down his bag and went to look around, when his father turned the corner, instant shock giving way to tearing eyes. Without a word, Tullius enveloped his son in a deep embrace, kissing his cheek and holding him tight. Cicero was stunned. His father had never shown him so much emotion.

"Where's Mother?" Cicero asked.

Tullius stepped back, looking at his son. After a moment, he pulled Cicero again into an embrace that made Cicero's stomach drop.

"Father, where is Mother?" Cicero asked, pushing his father off.

"You've been gone so long," Tullius said, hanging his head. "We wrote, but never heard."

"What do you mean? Where is Mother?" Cicero pressed.

"She passed, son. Your mother is dead."

Chapter Seven

Cicero awoke in darkness. He had always woken up early, but in the months since his return home, he'd been regularly waking well before first light. Like the typical Roman, Cicero rolled from bed and started his day with minimal preamble. Because of fire danger, food was rarely cooked in one's apartment, so after dressing, there was little reason to stay home. After quickly shaking off the cobwebs and dressing, Romans generally headed right out into the city to break their fast at a food stall and begin the activities of their day. Normally, Cicero would do the same, but as he finished dressing, he saw that it was still dark outside.

Cicero peered out the window into the black streets below. He supposed he had an hour before the sun rose and he could navigate the city, but he knew it could be longer.

Moving throughout the house, Cicero neatened and cleaned it well. As his father slept, Cicero stacked empty wine jugs in the corner and removed the empty vessel from his father's hand.

Looking outside again, Cicero realized it may be earlier than he'd thought, so he lit a candle and plucked a scroll from his shelf. Feeling hungry, Cicero popped a couple of olives in his mouth and ripped off a wedge of day-old bread. It was enough to sate his appetite until the kitchens opened below. The rest of the bread and olives he left for his father, hoping having only stale bread and olives to eat would be enough to motivate Tullius to leave the apartment at a better hour than what had become his norm.

Cicero yawned. What a cruel fate, he thought, that he should be so tired and yet completely unable to sleep. His insomnia was no great mystery because life was uncertain right now. Since returning to the city over a year ago, Cicero had studied the law and started soliciting as a lawyer, but outside of a few minor jobs, he had been unable to find consistent, well-paying work. It was this uncertainty about his future that kept Cicero up at night and, even crueler, woke him before the morning.

Complicating matters, a few weeks after Cicero returned to Rome, Sulla did the same, but he did not march his army into the city. That much Cicero was grateful for, but the strong man did everything else to solidify his power. With Sulla unrivaled as the most powerful man in Rome, the Senate avoided an occupation by Sulla's army by simply naming him dictator, a title typically only bestowed upon a leader for a single year and only in time of dire wartime need, when politics had to be thrust aside in favor of swift action. In Sulla's case, however, there was no war, and he took the title for life. Marius had taken similar autocratic measures when he was in control, and it was those actions that Cicero hoped to stop by joining Sulla's army. Indeed, he had stopped Marius, but Sulla went even further in using exactly the same tactic.

Since returning to Rome, Cicero had seen Marius's supporters purged from government and often from the city itself. Sulla was removing all his enemies and securing his place. Sulla also made the most of his unchecked power to push through government reforms and infrastructure repairs that had become bogged down in the partisan Senate. But Rome was a republic and in Cicero's mind, no amount of good deeds could overcome Sulla's attacks on the very structure of their society. Nonetheless, Cicero remained silent and anonymous as he worked to carve out a life for himself. Perhaps some years down the road, if Cicero could climb up the ladder into public life, he could work to keep the republic safe from such men, but until then he didn't want to end up on Sulla's list of enemies.

Cicero yawned as he finished reading the last lines of his scroll. He reached for the next one, but stopped as a welcome sight caught his eye. Peering out the window, he saw that dawn was on its way.

Sharp beams of sunlight cut through the shadows as Cicero made his way through streets and alleyways. A soft haze drifted through the morning air from the bakers' ovens and wood fires of the corner kitchens that churned out equal parts smoke and aroma.

Cicero walked through the city briskly. He was early, but he was also taking the long way to the courthouse square, so he felt the need to move quickly. He was taking the long way a lot lately; actually, he'd taken it every day this month.

Coming to the corner, Cicero slowed, as the reason for his new route passed by him. Terentia and Cicero met eyes and exchanged smiles. He had first seen her a few weeks ago, and he'd gone out of his way every day since to make sure he saw her again and again. Even so, he'd never actually spoken to her.

After the first sighting, Cicero asked around until he found out her name. He had never done anything like that before. Of course, he had also never felt anything like this before. Tall and elegant, Terentia was every bit the model of a young patrician woman. That's what scared Cicero about her the most. What could a woman like her find in a man like him? Cicero was more intelligent than any man he'd ever encountered, so if he couldn't find a reason for a beautiful young woman like Terentia to be interested in him, then he doubted there *was* one. Nonetheless, he added an extra half hour to his walk every morning just to see her. If nothing else, he knew he would enjoy that part of his day.

The courtyard outside the Forum was empty as Cicero set up his table in the usual spot. He was the first lawyer there and could have his pick of the area, but as he learned in his first days soliciting, the prime locations belonged to the more seasoned, wealthier lawyers. His area off to the side was not as desirable, but it was also safe from the stout plebeian men who worked for his competition.

Set up under an overhang of one of the perimeter buildings, Cicero wisely chose the one spot that had shade all day. It may not have been in the center of the action, but as summer appcroached and the days grew warmer, Cicero was grateful for the protective shade of his little space. He hoped the others wouldn't catch on and try to push him out.

The empty area around Cicero was vast and open and soon to be filled with countless lawyers, each barking to potential clients in search of legal representation. It was a loud, carnival atmosphere and one that did not suit Cicero. He knew the law as well as and probably better than any man out there, but he lacked the brash, rhetorical style to stand out in such a crowd. To this point he'd had only meager success establishing himself in a profession that, although built on the substance of law, somehow still valued style over all else.

Law in Rome was an entrepreneurial enterprise. There were no official qualifications or requirements nor was there a formal path of schooling to become a lawyer. In fact, as a technical matter, the profession was not even legally recognized, as citizens of Rome were expected to plead their own cases to earn the judgment of their peers. The precedent of self-representation went back to the early days of the republic, but as the laws grew in number and complexity, an industry of legal expertise sprouted organically with them.

Early on, law was practiced primarily by former senators as a public service in their retirement, but as those august men gave credence to the profession, others took it up as their vocation early in life. Though still not officially recognized, working as a lawyer had informally grown into a stepping-stone into public life. For a man without vast wealth or patrician blood, success in law meant not just an introduction to elite society, it also provided access to the masses who visited the public trials as a form of public entertainment. Though not as enthralling as theater, Romans of all ilk flocked to trials to learn about their friends and neighbors and enjoy the drama of legal strife.

Cicero did not much like the trial crowds, and had only argued one case in front of them, but such was a necessary evil in his quest to spark a political career. He enjoyed the law and the idea of being of service to others in their time of need, but what he really wanted was to be of service to the republic. He just needed to figure out how to turn the former into the latter.

As the first lawyers trickled into the courtyard, Cicero laid out his law scrolls and writing quill. He brought more materials than anyone else, something his shoulder reminded him of every night, but Cicero liked having the materials as a reference for clients. He had long since memorized the scrolls, but they looked nice and their presence informed the casual passerby that he was a serious lawyer. The youngest lawyer of the bunch by five years, Cicero looked even younger, so he had to do whatever he could to appear a bit more august. If it took a pile of scrolls that led to a sore shoulder, then so be it.

The real annoyance was the jeers Cicero got from the older lawyers. Having dealt with such slights all his life, Cicero's skin was already thick, so the hazing he got from his peers didn't bother him. What did bother him was the effect the ribbing had on business. Starting out as such a young man in law was hard enough, but it was nearly impossible to convince a potential client of his worth when the other lawyers hurled insults his way and mocked his inexperience. Cicero had twice the legal knowledge of the others, but it was hard to convince a potential client to entrust their legal fate to someone who was being chided by much older, more experienced men.

Most days, Cicero didn't get as much as a nibble from potential clients. The same lawyers tended to snatch up all the prime cases, so Cicero and the dregs of the lawyer corps fought for the scraps. In his first days, Cicero wasn't even in on those jobs. Quiet and cerebral, Cicero was put off by the idea of barking out solicitations to passing people. Why would someone hire a lawyer just because they were the loudest or the best salesman? But after a few days without even a look his way, it became clear that, in the face of barking sales pitches, the average lawyer seeker wasn't going to be swayed by a quiet respectful argument of the law. Cicero needed to figure out how to sell himself.

The learning curve was steep. Preamble and nuance was tossed aside, and Cicero learned to not just project his voice to the passers-by, but to read the person and intuit what would convince them. It had been months now and he'd needed every moment of that time, but Cicero was finally inuring himself to the process. No longer was he embarrassed to call out to a stranger or rattle off his qualifications. Even so, there were only so many jobs to go around.

"Hello, sir—" Cicero said, as a balding man passed by him with nary a look, making his way to an older lawyer instead. The day had been unusually busy. Perhaps last week's full moon had roused the populace into conflict, Cicero thought. But as busy as the day had been, by the late afternoon Cicero had yet to have someone return his solicitations with a single response.

"Are you looking for a lawy—"

"My name is Cice—"

"I'm the most knowledgeable lawyer in Rome—"

Every person that approached chose to keep walking, and Cicero realized he was the lone lawyer in the entire square that was not currently talking to a client. More embarrassed than discouraged, Cicero leaned against a column and took a breath.

Cicero had not eaten yet, so he opened his satchel and pulled out his lunch. Unfurling the cloth from a wedge of soft cheese, Cicero paired it with a grip of bread and took a small bite. The moment the salty cheese hit his palate, his mouth watered and his stomach rumbled as if his body needed food to remind it to be hungry. Cicero took a second, much larger bite, really savoring the experience—

"Are you a lawyer?"

Cicero looked up to see a beleaguered woman of forty standing before him. He chewed and searched in futility for the water jug he failed to bring. Finally, he choked down the bite, feeling it skid down his dry throat.

"Um…yes…I am," Cicero forced out the words, as he swallowed again and regained his composure.

"I am. I am versed in all manner of law. May I inquire as to the nature of your case?" Cicero said, slyly putting his lunch back into his bag.

"You seem kind of young," the woman said, her eyes wandering to other litigators.

Feeling he was losing her, Cicero straightened up. "I don't just seem that way, I am indeed the youngest man here. But I'm also the most knowledgeable. I'm a scholar and lifelong student of the law. I've learned more in my few years than most of colleagues have in their many," Cicero said. Such self-aggrandizement embarrassed him, but Cicero was inured to it enough that he could hide his discomfort to some degree.

The woman looked at Cicero a moment, then stretched out her hand. "My name is Caecillia," she said.

"A pleasure to make your acquaintance, Caecillia. I am Marcus Tullius Cicero. May I ask the nature of your legal case?" Cicero said.

Caecillia took a breath.

"Murder," she said.

Cicero paused.

"Alleged, of course," Caecillia said.

"Of course," Cicero said, barely able to contain his excitement. Murder cases were highly sought after and notoriously difficult to attain. The legal ins and outs were pretty simple, but the public interest was high. This was a real chance to make a name for himself!

"Can I ask the name of the accused?" Cicero asked.

"My husband, Sextus Roscius," Caecillia said. "But he didn't do it."

"No, of course not," Cicero responded. Cicero was being polite, but he also knew that murder cases were not always straightforward. Sometimes people were accused in error, or the complicated emotions of grief led to accidents being called murders. It was not uncommon for political battles to find their way into the court by way of false murder accusations. Whatever the reality, this was a major opportunity, and without a doubt the best he'd had.

"And the accuser?" Cicero asked.

Caecillia looked around, concerned.

"It's fine. You can tell me," he said, his interest peaked. Clearly this was an important case. He might be going up against a public figure.

"Lucius Sergius Catiline," Caecillia said.

Cicero's quill stopped.

"Catiline," he said.

"Yes. You know of him?" Caecillia asked.

Cicero sighed, "I do."

Cicero walked in somnambulant cadence, his unconscious mind navigating his body as his conscious brain mulled over the events of the afternoon. He'd had it in his hand. It was the job that would have given him a career—a real murder trial. But he had to turn it down because, as much as he disliked Catiline, Sulla would surely have seen it as a direct attack. Cicero knew he had no choice, but he still felt for Caecillia and her husband Roscius. She'd already been to every other lawyer in the square before coming to Cicero, and she'd gotten the same answer from each. Being her last choice was humbling, but Cicero mostly felt sick because he added to the helplessness of this poor couple's situation.

Normally, lawyers were safe from retribution from their opposition. But since Sulla had taken power in Rome, his foes had found themselves on proscription lists, which led to their unfortunate fates. In charge of those lists was Catiline, who had risen to take Sulla's side as his Number Two. So, while the other lawyers Caecillia approached didn't have the same baggage Cicero had with Catiline, they certainly knew the inherent danger in opposing Rome's second strongest man in trial. Whatever the case, Cicero's situation was even more tenuous. He had personal business with both Catiline and Sulla, so for ethical reasons he could not take this case. But if ethics were the real reason he couldn't help Caecillia and Roscius and it was all out of his hands, why was Cicero so sick to his stomach?

Just then, a graying man stumbled from an alleyway, the rowdy clatter of the drinking house he just stepped from following him into the street. As the man tripped and fell to his knees, Cicero helped him up.

"Come on, Father," Cicero said, steadying Tullius. "Let's get you home."

Cicero lay in bed, staring out the window. It was late. As much as sleep had been a problem recently, this was something worse. Getting home, Cicero made sure his father ate dinner, then hurried to get him into bed before the full day of drinking sent him into slumber at the table. Cicero had never known his father to drink, but the death of Helvia had hit Tullius hard, so when Cicero returned home, he found a broken man who looked like his father but acted nothing like him. Managing what was left of their remaining family land used to take up the bulk of his father's days. Now, with the land long since sold, Tullius whiled away his days drinking up what was left of the proceeds from the sale. Of course it bothered Cicero to see a once-proud man devolve into such a sad wretch and that had kept him up many nights, but it was not what was keeping him up tonight.

Occasionally, Cicero's mind wandered to Terentia, as daydreams of a life with her danced through his imagination. But it wasn't Terentia that was keeping him up either. It was Caecillia.

Cicero rolled to his other side, clamping his eyes shut. But for all his efforts to sleep, he couldn't stop thinking about having turned down the job. It was dishonorable. There was no other way to look at it. His issues with Sulla were a great excuse, but that didn't change the fact that he had turned his back on people who had asked for his help. As he struggled with his thoughts, they turned to the conversation he had with Caecillia.

"Please, I've been to everyone else already," Caecillia said. "There's no one else to go to." She didn't mean it as an insult and Cicero did not take offense, but it certainly showed where he stood in the pecking order of Roman lawyers.

"I've spoken to every lawyer who would give me the time, and none of them want to take up my husband's case," Caecillia continued.

"You're up against powerful people," Cicero said.

"And that is why we need help. Roscius didn't kill his father. He wasn't even near his father at the time of his death, but witnesses started coming forward saying he was. They're trying to steal the family land," Caecillia said.

"Because patricide voids the inheritance claim," he said.

"Yes. Exactly. Please, you can help us," Caecillia said, pleading.

Cicero rolled over in bed, opening his eyes to stare out through his window. He told Caecillia that he had a conflict of interest and could not help her. He even offered to help her find another lawyer, but Caecillia was too distraught to listen and wandered off, crying.

Cicero rolled back to his other side, hoping the new position would bring on the slumber he so dearly needed. It didn't. Instead, in his mind's eye he kept seeing Caecillia crying.

Cicero walked along his typical path to work, noticeably worse from the lack of sleep. He was unable to fall asleep, but he never missed work, so here he was, sluggish and dull, on his way to the Forum. Even so, Cicero would have loved to turn around and crawl back into bed. But he'd probably just lie there again, so there was no reason not to keep on toward work.

As he walked, Cicero's mind wandered. Maybe he had left his chance at a political career back in Sulla's tent. Maybe he had left his chance at *any* career back in that tent. Coming to a corner, Cicero's stomach dropped as he realized that he might be wasting his time trying to build a ladder into politics through law. With Sulla's power showing no signs of weakening, this would likely not be the last conflict he encountered with his former mentor. Despite all his planning and work, Cicero's journey into the law might have all been pointless. The thought scared him. Initially, practicing law was just a stepping-stone for Cicero's move into politics, but when faced with the thought that even law might be a fool's errand for him, he became disheartened. Without law, what would he have?

Turning the corner, Cicero rammed into someone. Head down and deep in thought, the impact sent Cicero stumbling to the ground without even seeing the other person. Gathering himself, Cicero grabbed his bag went to stand right back up, but stopped as the person he ran into stood above him, reaching out a hand. It was Terentia.

"I'm so sorry. I wasn't looking and…" Terentia said.

"No, no. It was my fault. I'm late for work and I wasn't paying attention," Cicero responded. "I apologize."

Cicero smiled at Terentia, then nerves got the best of him and he tensed up.

"I should get going though," Cicero said, picking his bag up from the ground.

"So soon?" Terentia said with a smile.

Behind Terentia, a stream of liquid fell from an apartment window into the road in a sick plop. Cicero knew the sound well, and motioned Terentia off to the side.

"Perhaps we can talk elsewhere," he said.

Cicero and Terentia sat in a corner food stall and talked. Cicero tried not to smile like the lovesick fool he was, but did a poor job of it. If she gave the faintest hint of coming to the end of what she had to say, he jumped in with another question, then sat back and enjoyed the response. Terentia was indeed of patrician birth, and her father was a former Senator and a major landowner in Cambia. She enjoyed going out to the country estate, but she said it got boring, so she preferred the city. Cicero learned about her brothers and sisters, the foods she liked, the jewelry she didn't. He just wanted to keep learning about her.

"But what about you?" she asked.

"I'm boring. I'd like to know more about you," Cicero said. "I'm serious."

"So am I."

"Where were you going in such a hurry?"

"The courts."

"But this isn't the way to the courts."

Cicero smiled. "Yeah, but I like the view this way," he said.

Terentia smiled and they enjoyed a quiet moment. Then, Terentia's eyes went wide with interest.

"Are you being sued?" Terentia asked.

"What?" Cicero said, confused.

"Is that why you're going to the courts? Is someone suing you? Can I come watch? I love trials," Terentia said.

Cicero laughed. "No. I'm a lawyer. At least, I think I am."

"What do you mean?" Terentia asked

"I don't know. I'm wondering if perhaps the law is not for me," Cicero said.

Terentia grimaced.

"What?" Cicero asked.

"I see you on your way every day and you seem so excited to get there. How could it possibly not be for you?"

"Well, recent events have made me reconsider my career choices," Cicero said.

Terentia looked at him a moment, really considering his words. "Then what drew you to it in the first place?" she asked.

Cicero considered.

"I want to use it to get into politics," Cicero said. "But maybe I need to find another way."

"Yes, but why?" Terentia asked.

"Why what?" Cicero responded.

"Why do you want to get into politics?" Terentia asked.

"For the republic. To help people," Cicero said matter-of-factly.

"Can't you help people as a lawyer?" Terentia asked.

Cicero paused, staring back. After a moment, he hung his head and Terentia grew concerned.

"Did I say something wrong?" she asked.

Cicero looked back at her. "No, you said exactly the right thing."

Cicero hurried up the third flight of stairs. It took him half the day, but he had finally found the address. Through all the activity, he had forgotten to eat and that bill was coming due as he lurched up the last of the steps.

Coming to the top, he caught his breath and moved down the hall. As he approached, a door opened and Caecillia stepped out. She looked at Cicero, confused.

"Do you still need a lawyer?" Cicero asked.

Chapter Eight

"What can you tell me about your father?" Cicero asked. "Did he have any enemies? Anyone that might want him done ill?"

Sextus Roscius stared off, deep in thought, but not about Cicero's query.

"Sextus, are you listening?" Cicero asked.

Sextus looked back with a blank stare. "What?" Sextus asked.

Seated across from Roscius at the rickety wooden table dominating the small one-room apartment Sextus and Caecillia occupied, Cicero rubbed at his temples in frustration. With just a few weeks to prepare for the trial, they had worked as hard as possible, but Cicero could not help but worry it would not be enough. Sextus's distant stares only made him more concerned.

Broad-shouldered and rough-hewn, Sextus cut an imposing figure, but his weary eyes betrayed a broken spirit. After a difficult few months since his father's death, the powerfully built man of hard countryside work was looking worn and vulnerable.

"You must stay focused, Sextus," Caecillia said, putting a hand to Sextus's shoulder.

"Yes, of course," Sextus said, looking from Caecillia to Cicero. "You were saying?"

"Your father...who could have wanted this done to him?" Cicero asked.

"Nobody," Sextus responded.

Cicero and Caecillia sighed.

"What?" Sextus asked. "It's the truth."

"But that doesn't help your case, dear," Caecillia said.

"Well, maybe Catiline is behind it all," Sextus said. "I mean, he's the one accusing me and all."

"Yes, but why would Catiline accuse you?" Cicero said.

"Like you said," Sextus responded. "For the land."

"But how would he even know about you or your father?" Cicero said. "Surely there's someone feeding him information that is either against your father or against you. This is no small accusation, Sextus. Your father is dead and you stand accused of patricide, a crime that, if you are found guilty, would see you beaten to pulp, sewn into a leather bag, and tossed into the Tiber. Perhaps someone else was interested in the property."

"Me," Sextus said.

Cicero and Caecillia slumped.

"What?" Sextus said. "It's true. I've always wanted the land and my father made sure it was to be mine upon his death."

"But that won't help convince the judges of your innocence, dear," Caecillia said.

A straightforward, earnest man of the country, Roscius lacked the situational intelligence and the savvy that came with living in Rome. Perhaps, Cicero considered, this was why he chose to remain on the farms as a caretaker instead of moving to the city with his father. But the reality didn't matter much if Cicero couldn't figure out an angle with which to defend Roscius at trial.

At home on his father's lands, Roscius oversaw the ten high-producing farms, and he did a quality job of it. The land was Sextus's birthright and Cicero wanted to make sure Sextus would be able to retain it for generations to come. The elder Roscius was not a particularly political man and had supported Sulla in the past, so there was no reason for Sulla's Number Two, Catiline, to push this through for political gain. Plus, if Sulla wanted either Sextus the Elder or Younger dead, he could have just placed them on the proscribed list and they would have been killed months ago in the purges, along with the rest of Sulla's political enemies. But Cicero had checked and neither man was ever placed on the list. So, if Sextus had not killed his father and there was no reason for Sulla to want him dead for political reasons, either Sextus the Elder had an enemy nobody knew about, or someone was after the land.

Of course, there was another possibility: Sextus the Younger could be guilty. Cicero hated the thought. Over the past few weeks he'd really come to like Sextus. Sextus was a simple man and seemed as honest and loyal as anyone Cicero had ever known. But anything was possible, and Cicero's job wasn't to determine guilt or innocence, but to provide his client with the best defense possible. Nonetheless, he did not take the case for the money; he took it to keep an innocent man from losing his life.

"I know we've gone over it already, but Sextus was not even in the city at the time of his father's death," Caecillia said.

"It doesn't matter," Cicero said. "If Sextus paid someone to commit the crime, then he is responsible for it."

"But I didn't pay anyone anything," Sextus said, raising his voice.

"But they're going to say you did," Cicero said. "The trick is finding out why this was done and that should tell us who did it. Who do you think they will call as witnesses?"

"I don't know," Sextus said. "Could be anyone."

"Well, if you can think of anyone, let me know tomorrow," Cicero said. "Only the prosecution may call witnesses, so it would benefit us to be as prepared as possible for whoever they call."

Cicero peered out at the waning sun. He perked up, realizing the hour was late.

"I need to go," Cicero said. "I'll meet you both in the Forum tomorrow, and we can enter court together." Cicero paused and thought for a moment. "Just make sure you think of everything that could be brought up tomorrow. Any little family squabble could be brought up, so there is nothing too small."

"Yes, of course," Roscius said, then paused and considered. "What do you think our chances are?"

Cicero looked back, not wanting to tell him the truth.

"That bad, huh?" Roscius said. "Well, at least the farms are being taken care of, even if I can't be there to do it."

"That's good. Try to stay positive—" Cicero stopped. "Who's running the operation right now?"

"My cousins, Capito and Magnus," Roscius said.

"And you get on well with both?" Cicero asked.

Caecillia perked up. "Do you think they could be involved?"

"Do they have a reason to be?" Cicero asked.

"No, of course not," Roscius said. "They're family."

"I've seen family do worse," Cicero said. "Besides, you're family and that hasn't stopped you from being accused."

Roscius nodded sullenly.

"They could be, but they aren't the ones who bought the land," Caecillia said.

Cicero perked up. "The land was already auctioned? That shouldn't happen until after the trial."

"Catiline pushed it through," Caecillia said.

"Who bought it?" Cicero asked.

Roscius shrugged. "Catiline."

Cicero kicked food around his plate with his fingers, staring off into oblivion. Seated at a long dining table in a vast, open space of Terentia's patrician parents' villa, Cicero's body was present, but his mind was already arguing his case before the court, cycling through in his head over and over again.

"Are you not well, son?" Terentia's father asked.

Cicero perked up, looking over to see Terentia and her parents staring at him.

"Perhaps the meal is not to your liking?" Terentia's father continued, nodding toward Cicero's untouched food.

"Oh, no. The food is quite lovely. Really," Cicero said.

When courting Terentia, Cicero had spent much of the time with her family, but made little progress developing a rapport with them. They were cordial enough, but he could feel their reluctance about their daughter wanting to marry a lowly provincial.

"Cicero's trial begins tomorrow," Terentia said.

"Oh, dear. What are you on trial for?" Terentia's mother asked.

"Mother, no, he's representing someone at trial. I've told you all about it," Terentia said.

"Ah, yes, the big trial. This is your first, correct?" Terentia's father asked.

"I've argued a case before, but this is the biggest. I apologize for being distracted," Cicero said.

"Nonsense, it's fine. But it must be nerve-racking knowing you'll be up in front of all those people tomorrow," Terentia's father said. "I imagine it is tough to stay focused knowing they're all judging you by everything you say."

Cicero smiled, looking on the faces of the all the people currently judging him.

"It is," Cicero said, "but I owe it to my client to remain calm and collected. It's *his* life on the line after all."

"His life? Oh dear. What's the charge?" Terentia's mother asked.

Cicero gulped. "Patricide," he said.

Terentia's father's fake interest in Cicero immediately turned to sour suspicion. "Patricide?" Terentia's father pressed. "Is that some kind of joke?"

"No, sir," Cicero said, treading carefully. "No one else would dare represent Sextus and—"

"And it's clear why," Terentia's father said. "I mean, who would actually want to represent such a vile creature as someone who would kill their own father?"

"Well," Cicero said, "He's only accused of the crime, sir—"

"Accused?" Terentia's father said. "Nobody would dare make up an accusation such as that. This Sextus character should be tossed right in the Tiber. I see no reason to waste everyone's time with a trial. And I certainly see no reason to muddy my family's name with such business, either."

Cicero stiffened and started to retort, but bit his lip when he caught Terentia's gaze.

"Perhaps we should talk of something else," Terentia's mother said.

"Yes, perhaps we should," Terentia's father said, glaring at Cicero.

88

~

As servants cleared the table, Cicero grabbed his things by the door. He was exhausted from all the work for the impending trial, but somehow more so from the rigors of the meal he just stumbled through.

"I'm sorry about my father," Terentia said, trailing behind.

"It's fine," Cicero said. "He's right, it's not a glamorous case."

Terentia's face dropped. "I thought you said it was a stepping-stone," Terentia said. "That it would propel you into politics."

Cicero read her concern and adeptly buried his own. "It will," he said. "I was just bellyaching. It's a fine case and it will do me, er...*us* well." Cicero forced a smile onto his face. "But I should get going. The trial starts tomorrow, so I have to be up early."

Chapter Nine

Cicero clasped his hands, hoping that each would obscure if not quell the shaking of the other. He had once thought he'd known what it was like to have trouble sleeping, but with the case approaching, the past few days had taught him how lucky he'd been. But for all his lack of rest, Cicero was not the least bit tired, and the anxiety of what was to come, he suspected, was responsible for that. Even so, he wished his hands would stop shaking.

Taking a breath, Cicero looked around the large courtyard before him. For the case he'd worked on before, he had little more than a hallway within which he was to present his arguments. It was a petty property dispute, so the public was not very interested in it and little room was needed for viewers of the proceedings. Today, however, as he looked out from his table, he had an entire square of the Forum to present to.

Set up in the open sun, the courtyard was off to the side of the Forum, but vast enough to fit more than a hundred spectators in relative comfort. The one saving grace was that the spectators would be behind him, so he wouldn't have to feel their stares the entire time. He would, however, have to hear all their reactions, good and bad.

At the fore of the courtyard sat a series of chairs atop the stairway to a pillared building, with a single chair at the bottom of the stairs. The chairs at the top would be for the judges, who would decide the fate of Sextus. The chair at the bottom would be for the attending praetor, who would oversee the case for the government and see that a fair hearing was held.

To Cicero's right was the seating for the lawyer of the accuser. Cicero had heard murmurs about his potential rival, but nothing had been confirmed. Whoever the other lawyer was, Cicero knew he would be far more experienced and far more known by the crowds of onlookers and the judges themselves. It was a lot of pressure, but that was why Cicero had come early. Sitting in the space without anyone there allowed him to get a feel for it all in hopes of dulling some of the fear of the unknown that haunted him. But soon people would arrive, so he needed to gather his wits and prepare.

Cicero closed his eyes and took a deep, centering breath. At first his mind went over his opening argument and his goals for the case, but it soon trailed off into thoughts of Terentia and his father. Cicero saw himself back on the road to Rome. The city was before him, but as he walked, it seemed to move farther and farther away from him. He began to run, but the city's departure seemed to hasten too. He dropped into a dead sprint as the darkness of night deepened behind him, threatening to overtake him…

A hand set upon Cicero's shoulder, jolting him awake and Cicero looked up to see a tall, august man with a luxuriant beard standing before him.

"Sorry. Just wanted to introduce myself," the man said.

Cicero knew the man immediately as Gaius Erucius, perhaps the greatest prosecutor in Rome. Cicero realized right then that he had underestimated the desires of the powers-that-be that his client not be acquitted of this crime. Already filled with self-doubt and concern that he was in over his head, Cicero now knew just how desperately deep the waters were.

"Sorry to cause you such fright," Erucius said, smirking. This was a man who knew his station and used it to maximum effect against lesser lawyers.

"Cicero, correct?" Erucius asked, but didn't wait for an answer. "I just wanted to introduce myself, since it appears we'll be arguing against each other."

Erucius extended his hand to Cicero and said, "Sorry again to frighten you so."

"No need for apology, I was just going over my arguments," Cicero said with a little bluster of his own.

"I'm not sure how much it will matter, but I didn't want you to miss out on the event," Erucius said as he turned to leave.

"You're not sticking around?" Cicero asked.

Erucius smiled smarmily. "No," Erucius said, "I just came to make sure you made it to the right court."

Erucius continued out of the courtyard and Cicero looked at the empty space around him. Had he come to the wrong place? Cicero quickly packed his things and stepped outside.

Cicero found himself in a square more than twice the size of the one that had already made him so nervous. Columns rose up along three sides, surrounding a courtyard that opened to a staircase leading up to one of the most imposing buildings of the Forum. The space was large but, even worse, it was crowded with not just spectators but the judges and presiding praetor, Marcus Fannius, as well. And they were all looking at Cicero as he swallowed his pride and hurried in with Erucius leading the way.

"Not to worry, folks," Erucius said to the masses. "I have found the long-lost lawyer for the defense."

With jeers and laughter following him, Cicero approached the defense table, spilling out all his materials onto it. Sextus and Caecillia, already seated, grabbed the scrolls to keep them from falling to the ground.

"Is everything fine?" Caecillia asked.

"Yes," Cicero said. "I just went to the wrong—" Cicero paused, seeing the man who had pointed him to the other court area seated behind Erucius. Cicero grumbled under his breath, "Let's just worry about what happens from here on out."

"Thank you for gracing us with your presence, Mr. Cicero," Praetor Fannius said looking down from his pedestal. "Can I assume that you are actually prepared to argue your case today?"

"I am, sir," Cicero said. "I apologize for my tardiness."

"Well, from what I've seen, this should be a short case, so it should matter not," Fannius said.

Cicero looked over at the judges sitting to the side. With the praetor already making his feelings clear, how could the judges possibly give Sextus fair consideration?

"Mr. Erucius, I know you're always prepared. Please get us started," Fannius said.

Erucius stood and walked to the fore, his chest puffed out. He was the picture of calm confidence, and the crowd cheered as he waved and smiled to them with his signature smirk.

"Gentleman…Romans," Erucius said, "I stand before you today as not just a prosecutor here to argue a case, but as a son and a father and a Roman citizen who is horrified and disgusted by the crime you are all about to hear described. Patricide."

Erucius stepped before Sextus, looking coldly upon him. It was all theater, but Cicero could not help but be impressed with the man's delivery.

"Yes," Erucius continued, "you heard that right. Patricide: the murder of a father by a son. Perhaps the single most vile, hateful crime a Roman can commit. And this is the man who committed it." Erucius pointed at Sextus, who was just feet from him.

"Sextus Roscius the Younger," Erucius said. "A man with such low moral fiber that he killed the man who gave him life. His own father!" Erucius exclaimed, thrusting his hands up in convincing but certainly feigned anger.

"Think about that," Erucius continued. "Sextus Roscius the Elder, a man who worked tirelessly to attain and build up vast lands that helped feed and nourish his son, suffered death at the hands of that same son. And in one of the cruelest forms of hate, Sextus the Younger killed his father so as to take the very land his father used to support him in the first place. Please, just think about that. I know it is painful to imagine such an atrocity, but we owe the deceased that final kindness as we work to bring justice to the son who killed him."

Erucius turned to the judges, a group of older men, each of senatorial rank and each looking much like Erucius himself. "And I ask you, our honored judges, to think about your own fathers and sons and then think again about Sextus Roscius and the kind of man who would feel nothing about killing his own father. That is no man that deserves to live. That is no Roman."

Erucius looked on the judges, pausing for dramatic effect.

"So," Erucius continued, "I ask you to listen to the tale of lies and deceit, and jealousy and murder, and all the horrible details of this crime that I will tell you about during the course of this trial. And then, after you have heard all the unfortunate details, after you have seen the world through the eyes of evil, after you have seen the awful hate that causes a son to strike down his own father, I will ask you to hold Sextus Roscius responsible for his heinous act, and I will ask you to do the only sane thing that one can do when faced with such unspeakable evil…"

Erucius turned, half-facing the massive audience and again paused for dramatic effect. "I will ask you to dispatch this murderer just as he dispatched his father."

After a brief moment of silence, the crowd erupted into cheers and applause. Erucius stepped back to his table, offering Cicero a smirk.

"Mr. Cicero, it is your turn to address the court," Fannius said.

Cicero looked down at his hands, which shook worse than before. Sextus and Caecillia saw Cicero's hands and traded concerned glances, as Cicero did not move.

After a few moments, Erucius looked over at the unmoving Cicero, then to the audience. "It would appear that Mr. Cicero is as certain of his client's guilt as the rest of us are," Erucius said with a chuckle.

"Mr. Cicero, it is your turn to argue," the praetor said, but Cicero did not stir.

Caecillia leaned in toward Cicero. "Are you all right?"

Cicero shut his eyes and took a breath. He stood.

"I imagine that you are all marveling as to why it is that when the most eminent orators and most noble men are still seated that I should be the one to advocate for Sextus Roscius," Cicero said.

"I have neither age, nor ability, nor influence. I am no one to be compared to those who are sitting still. Yet, here I stand.

"Understand, though, that all these men whom you see present at this trial believe that a man ought to be defended against all injury contrived against him, but through the sad state of the times they dare not defend him themselves. So it comes to pass that they are present here because they are attending to their business, but they are silent because they are afraid of danger.

"Am I the boldest of all these men of the law? No," Cicero continued. "Am I more attentive to my duties to the law? I am not. Then why am I the one standing in defense of Citizen Roscius? If any one of my more experienced, more revered colleagues had taken the call, I never would have had the chance to speak today. But here I stand as advocate to this cause. Not because I am the most able, but because I was the only person left."

The crowd chuckled.

"Quiet. Quiet, please," Fannius said, arms outstretched, motioning the horde to calm.

"No, no. It's fine. I understand why you laugh," Cicero continued. "It is a laughable situation and certainly one that has humbled me in my pursuits. Because, you see, I almost didn't stand for Sextus Roscius either. Not because I did not think I could argue his case with skill and not because I doubted his innocence, which, I can assure you all, is a simple matter of fact. But, you see, I am no different than all my colleagues in this matter, because I first chose not to accept this cause for the same reason. *Fear.* Fear of Sextus Roscius's accuser, Lucius Sergius Catiline, or as most know him, Catiline, the right hand of Dictator Lucius Cornelius Sulla."

The crowd gasped as Cicero looked around to the spectators, the judges, and finally Erucius. Erucius was taken aback by his counterpart's brash confidence.

"To understand the fear surrounding Citizen Roscius's cause, we need focus on one thing: *Qui bono?* Who benefits? And when you understand the answer to that question, you will understand why no lawyer would take this case, and you will understand why the august Erucius would agree to prosecute when he has no evidence to present. *Qui bono?* Who benefits?" Cicero said, pausing to give his words a moment to sink in.

"Let me tell you of the matters of this case," Cicero continued. "First, we have Sextus Roscius the Elder, a man of means, living in Rome off the proceeds of his ten prosperous farms in the Ameria province. But Roscius the Elder was struck down in an alley, waylaid by a saber, and left to bleed out in the streets. Our respected prosecutor, Erucius, will tell you this is a crime of passion, perpetrated by Sextus Roscius the Younger to gain ownership of his father's lands. But Roscius the Younger was already running the operation of his father's farms and was in line to inherit them eventually anyway. Why murder his father now? Remember that question, because Erucius will have no answer for it, because he has no evidence. But if Roscius the Younger did not commit the crime, who did? And I can answer that question for you: *Qui bono?*

"As a matter of law," Cicero said, "Roscius the Younger has lost his family land. No person accused of patricide is eligible to inherit the estate of the father they killed. So, why would he commit this crime?"

Cicero paced toward the twenty judges, who looked on stone-faced.

"The answer is simple: he didn't," Cicero said. "Roscius the Younger did not hate his father, nor did he benefit from his father's death. So, as a simple matter of logic, he had no reason to kill him. And, despite what Erucius will tell you, this was not a crime of passion, because Roscius the Younger was not in Rome at the time of his father's death."

Cicero stepped before the judges, looking on each as he rounded out his argument. "No," Cicero said. "There was no passion in this crime. This was an organized, thought-out attack on a citizen of Rome and, as you will see, the motivations all lead to a single man. The corrupt arm of the Dictator of Rome, Catiline."

Gasps came from the crowd as the judges shifted nervously in their seats, their stone faces cracking with consternation. Cicero paused a moment, his calm showing a deep confidence that caused even Erucius to grow concerned.

"But these are not baseless claims," Cicero continued. "Erucius has plenty of those already. No, the path to Catiline's involvement is clear, and we need only ask the same single question to get us there: *Qui bono?* Who benefited?"

Cicero looked on each judge in turn, finally relenting and stepping back to his seat, passing an angry, red-faced Erucius. As Cicero took his seat, Sextus nodded to him with equal parts admiration and gratitude. Caecillia smiled through thankful tears. Cicero breathed out, relieved.

Capito Roscius took a seat at a chair in the middle of the square. The first witness at the trial, the shifty, slender man fidgeted as he tried to remain calm among the sea of people peering on him. Cicero looked Capito over. Though slender, Capito's arms were corded with the tight muscles of a workingman and his skin was dark and aged from years of sun exposure. Despite these marks of a life of labor, he was wearing clean, expensive robes and shiny, new bronze bracelets that a laborer should be unable to afford.

Erucius approached Capito with his usual confident swagger.

"Please state your name for the attending," Erucius said.

"I am Capito Roscius."

"Thank you, Mr. Roscius. And will you tell us your relation to the defendant?"

"He is my cousin."

"Your cousin?"

"Yes."

"So, then Sextus Roscius is accused of killing your uncle?"

"Yes, sir. And Sextus Roscius the Elder was a fine man."

"Indeed he was. I'm sorry for your loss, and I'm sorry that you must be here while you are still in mourning."

"Justice must be served."

To the side, Sextus huffed out confused breaths. Finally, he leaned to Cicero. "He barely knew my father. Why would he say that?" Sextus asked.

"It's fine," Cicero said, waving Sextus to calm. "We'll have our turn to talk with him."

"So," Erucius continued, "as the cousin of the defendant, I assume you've spent much time with him."

"Yes, sir," Capito said. "We've worked together on his father's farms for years. He's like a brother to me."

Sextus sighed. "We've hardly talked to each other," he said, looking again to Cicero. This time the exchange was loud enough to draw Erucius's eyes. Cicero calmed Sextus, motioning him to stop speaking.

"Like brothers?" Erucius said. "So, as brothers, Roscius probably confided in you. Did he ever tell you how he felt about his father?"

"He hated him," Capito responded.

Roscius bolted up from his chair. "Lies! He's lying," Roscius cried out.

Praetor Fannius motioned sternly to Roscius. "Quiet. This is a court of law." The praetor then looked to Cicero and barked, "Control your client, sir."

Cicero put a calming hand to Sextus and nodded at him to sit. "You cannot do that," Cicero said.

"But he's lying," Sextus said.

"Yes," Cicero said. "But yelling so does not prove such to anyone." Sextus relented with a nod and slumped down into his chair.

Erucius smirked at Cicero, then looked toward the gallery. "Such a temper," Erucius said. "I suppose we shouldn't be surprised given the heinous nature of his crime."

Cicero hanged his head. It was not a good showing for Roscius.

Erucius looked back to Capito. "I apologize for the defendant's outburst," he said. "But I suppose his inability to control his anger is something you've grown accustomed to. Have you ever witnessed Sextus lash out at his father like that?"

"To his face? No," Capito said. "But Sextus told me of his wishes to see his father dead."

Sextus went to stand again, but Cicero put his hand to his arm, reminding Sextus to stay calm.

"He wished him dead?" Erucius asked. "Whatever for?"

"His father banished him to the farms out in the backwater of Ameria while he went to live here in Rome," Capito said. "Sextus hated him for forcing him to live out there."

"So," Erucius said, "Sextus hated living in Ameria, but his father controlled the wealth, so Sextus had no choice. That is, unless his father died." Erucius looked again to the gallery, playing up the moment with an actor's skill. "Qui bono indeed."

Erucius nodded smugly to Cicero as he took his seat.

Praetor Fannius looked to Cicero. "Do you wish to examine the witness, Mr. Cicero?" he asked.

Cicero patted Sextus on the arm and stood. "Yes, Praetor, I have but a few questions."

Cicero approached Capito, looking at the man with silent, probing eyes. Capito, thoroughly unnerved, broke into a sweat.

"Good day, Mr. Capito," Cicero said. "I'm sorry about the loss of your uncle. When did you first find out about his death?"

"The next day," Capito said.

"And where were you when you got word?" Cicero asked.

"On his farm in Ameria the morning after my uncle's murder," Capito said. "My cousin sent word from Rome."

"The next morning in Ameria?" Cicero said. "That's quite fast."

Capito shrugged.

"Interesting. So, you say that Sextus Roscius the Younger told you that he hated Ameria and held ill will to his father because he was forced to live in such a vile area," Cicero said.

"Not ill will. He wished him dead," Capito retorted, covering anxiety with antagonism.

"So you say," Cicero said, staring Capito deep in the eyes. "But what is so bad about Ameria?" Cicero looked on Capito a moment, as if he actually wanted him to answer. "Sure, Rome is the great center of our world, but it is not the only wonderful place. Ameria is renowned for its beautiful landscape and clean air and water. It's hardly a punishment."

"So says you," Capito barked back.

"No, Mr. Capito," Cicero retorted. "So say many of the members of our corps of judges here. I'm not sure if you're aware of this, but many of them have estates in Ameria. But I suppose they were forced to buy those as a punishment, right, Mr. Capito?"

Capito scowled back. The anger only emboldened Cicero.

"But I'm not worried about your characterization of Ameria," Cicero said. "I'm worried about your testimony about these conversations with the defendant. Was there anyone else present for these conversations?"

Capito looked to Erucius. Erucius gestured at Capito to look away. Cicero smirked and played to the gallery. "Excuse me, Mr. Capito, but I believe you are the one that had these conversations, not Mr. Erucius."

The crowd chuckled.

Finally, Capito looked to Cicero, anger now unvarnished. "We were alone," he barked.

"So," Cicero continued. "Your testimony is that you were alone when the defendant told you he hated his father for banishing him to the beautiful countryside? Were you also alone when he told you he wished his father dead?"

Capito nodded.

"Excuse me?" Cicero prodded.

"Yes," Capito barked.

"So," Cicero said. "This is just your word against that of Sextus Roscius?"

Capito just stared back.

"Well, that is concerning," Cicero said, as he moved to his seat.

Capito went to stand, but Cicero stopped and turned back. "Oh, just one more thing," Cicero said, as Capito slumped back down.

"I was noticing your hands," Cicero said. "They seem rough and rugged."

"Yeah, well, some of us have to work for a living," Capito said.

"That's right. You're a workingman, aren't you? A field hand," Cicero said.

"I was," Capito said, boasting.

"Does that mean you have a new job?" Cicero asked.

"I am the caretaker," Capito said.

"I'm surprised that a working man like yourself was able to make the acquaintance of such a high-ranking citizen as Catiline," Cicero said.

"What do you mean?" Capito asked, growing concerned.

"Well, he's the new owner of the land, yes?" Cicero asked.

Capito looked to Erucius.

"Dear boy," Cicero said to the older man, "do you need Erucius to give you your answers?"

Capito looked back to Cicero, frustrated by the minuscule young man treating him like a child. Finally, he answered. "Yes, he owns it now, but I had never met him before."

"So, you work for Catiline now, right?" Cicero confirmed.

"Yes, I do," Capito barked. "I'm the caretaker and operator of the farms. What of it?"

"Farms?" Cicero continued. "How many of your uncle's former farms?"

"Ten."

"Ten? Well, I have to say that that strikes me as odd," Cicero said, feigning confusion. "I mean, here you are, a simple farmhand, yet when your uncle mysteriously dies and your cousin is forced to give up all claims to the land, the new owner decides to make a farmhand—one that he's never met—a caretaker to not one, but all ten farms."

"So?" Capito snarled.

"So…I'd say that is an interesting turn of events," Cicero said, looking at Capito. "Your new robe and bracelets are beautiful, by the way. I don't suppose you would have been able to afford such items as just a farmhand, would you?"

Cicero looked on the once-confident Capito a moment, then to the gallery.

"Qui bono."

Erucius marched around the courtyard, playing to the audience, seemingly unaffected by Cicero's prior performance. Before him sat a new witness, Magnus Roscius. Also a cousin to Sextus, Magnus shared many of the same working man's physical traits as Capito, but he also carried an urban edge to him that could only be attained in the streets of Rome.

"And so you were the one to identify your uncle's body?" Erucius asked.

"I was," Magnus said. "I worked for Sextus the Elder here in Rome, and when he didn't come home in the evening, I grew concerned and went looking for him. A crowd had already formed around his body by the time I showed up."

"And did you start asking around about who was responsible?" Erucius asked.

"No," Magnus said.

"No?" Erucius asked, really playing up his faux confusion for the crowd. "But you'd just discovered that your uncle had been viciously murdered. Why wouldn't you want to find out who did it?"

"Because I already knew who did it," Magnus declared, then pointed to Sextus. "My cousin."

"So, you suspected Sextus Roscius the Younger of his father's murder?" Erucius asked.

"No."

"No? What do you mean?"

"I mean, I didn't suspect him. I *knew* it was him."

"How did you know?"

"Because he'd asked me to do it for him," Magnus said to gasps from those in attendance.

"He'd asked you?" Erucius asked, as if he hadn't known Magnus was going to say as much.

"He did," Magnus said. "He was very concerned. I tried to stick near him and keep him safe in case his son tried something. Unfortunately, he'd left that day before I'd realized he was gone. My cousin's goons must have known I wasn't around and chose then to strike."

Erucius put his hand to Magnus's shoulder. "It wasn't your fault. Your scheming cousin's hate would have found a way no matter what. Thank you for your words today."

Erucius turned and returned to his seat.

Cicero waited a moment, simply looking on Magnus. Finally, he stood and approached the witness.

"I'm sorry for your loss, Magnus," Cicero said.

Magnus, steeled for battle, was taken off guard by the pleasantry. He mumbled out, "Thank you."

"You worked for your uncle for many years. You must have been close," Cicero said.

"Very."

"And what were you doing prior to working for your uncle?"

"I did a lot of things."

"Were you ever a gladiator?"

Magnus sat up proudly. "I was."

"A gladiator," Cicero said with theatrical surprise. "Well, your uncle must have felt safe with you by his side."

"I'm sure he did," Magnus said.

"Well, except for his last night, that is," Cicero said, as Magnus glared at him. "But, I guess he sneaked out without you, so that's hardly your fault. Were you his only guard?"

"I wasn't his guard. I worked collecting on his accounts here in Rome. He didn't keep guards around," Magnus said.

"He didn't have any guards?" Cicero asked.

"No," Magnus said.

"Seems a bit odd for a man of means who knows his son is out to kill him to not only have no guards, but to leave without someone like you that could keep him safe," Cicero said.

"Is there a question coming?" Magnus said snidely.

"Yes. How many people have you killed?" Cicero asked.

"Excuse me?" Magnus said.

"Praetor, please," Erucius said, as he stood. "He should not be talking to the witness as if he is the defendant."

"Is this going somewhere, Mr. Cicero?" Praetor Fannius asked.

"The witness said he was a gladiator," Cicero said. "I would just like to do my due diligence and find out his skill level, and I believe the number of men he's killed speaks to such."

Fannius nodded to Magnus, bidding him to answer. Magnus stared at Cicero a moment, then puffed out his chest. "Ten."

"Ten!" Cicero exclaimed. "That is impressive. And how many have you killed since your time as a gladiator?"

Erucius leaped from his seat, barking to the praetor in a frothy rage, "How dare Mr. Cicero make these implications!"

"What implications?" Cicero asked, feigning ignorance.

Praetor Fannius motioned for quiet. "Unless you have some evidence to present, Mr. Cicero, stick to the matters at hand."

Cicero nodded to Fannius, "Understood, sir."

Cicero looked back to Magnus. "Magnus, your cousin Capito mentioned to us that he received word from Rome about his uncle's death. Was it you that sent the courier?"

"Yes," Magnus said. "Notifying family seemed the decent thing to do."

"I agree," Cicero said. "But it seems a little odd that Capito was the only family member you notified."

Magnus stared silently back, not comfortable being talked to like this from a man he could easily kill with his bare hands.

"Do you know how long it takes to ride to Ameria?" Cicero asked.

"What?" Magnus asked, confused.

"I'll answer," Cicero said. "It's a full day with the best of conditions and the sturdiest of steed. And I think that's important, because you said you didn't come upon your Uncle's body until evening, well after it had been discovered in the streets and yet you were able to send word to Ameria and get it there in half a day. It would seem your courier either knows a new method of travel, or you knew about the murder well before you have said."

Magnus scowled.

Erucius stood, pleading to Fannius, "Praetor, please. These are baseless insinuations. Mr. Cicero is treating this witness as if he's the one on trial and not the murderer Sextus Roscius the Younger."

"These are not baseless claims," Cicero said. "The heart of this case is qui bono. Who benefitted from this crime? I am working to answer exactly that question."

Fannius considered a moment, finally relenting. "Continue, Mr. Cicero," he said. "But stick to the facts."

"Yes, sir," Cicero said to Fannius, then looked to Magnus. "I have just one more question, Magnus. You said that you worked for your uncle collecting on his investments here in Rome. What do you do now?"

Magnus paused and looked to Erucius.

"Magnus," Cicero said. "It appears you have the same ailment that caused your cousin to keep looking to Erucius for answers. Do you not know how you make a living?"

Magnus huffed, "I am a land owner."

"A land owner?" Cicero said. "Well, congratulations. May I ask where this land is?"

Enraged, Magnus stared Cicero down. Finally, he swallowed the scorn and relented. "Ameria," he said.

"Ameria? Is it your uncle's land?"

"Yes."

"How much did you pay for it?"

Magnus gritted his teeth.

"Oh, and I should remind you," Cicero said, getting a little cocky. "I can check on the ownership transfer for the property, so please try to be accurate, sir."

Magnus huffed out angry breaths, finally barking out, "I didn't pay for it."

"You didn't pay for it? How did you obtain it then?" Cicero asked, his confidence growing.

"It was a gift," Magnus snarled.

"What a lovely gift. Who was it from?" Cicero asked.

Magnus again looked to Erucius.

Cicero smiled at the exchange, then looked to Fannius. "Praetor Fannius, would you mind guiding the witness toward his duties here?"

"Answer the question, Mr. Roscius," Fannius said.

Magnus paused, then finally under his breath, he said, "Catiline."

"Catiline?" Cicero said, projecting Magnus's answer to the courtyard. "The very man who brought charges against the defendant?"

Erucius stood. "Praetor, this trial is about patricide, not real estate."

"No," Cicero said, swelling with confidence. "This trial is about qui bono. Who benefitted from the murder of Sextus Roscius the Elder? It is clear that it was not the defendant who benefitted, but his cousins. It was Mr. Capito Roscius and Mr. Magnus Roscius who, even if they did not murder Elder Roscius themselves, certainly used his mysterious death to take a deal to Catiline, who then used his stature to accuse my client and negate his right of inheritance."

Cicero looked to the row of judges. "This trial is about corruption and blackmail. It is about a clear pattern of behavior that sought but one end: to attain this valuable property through murder."

"Like when Sextus murdered his older brother?" Magnus barked.

Cicero stopped dead in his tracks. "Excuse me?" Cicero said.

"Did you not know Sextus's brother, the rightful heir of his father's estate, was killed last year?" Magnus said.

"Hang on," Cicero said, as he appealed to Fannius. "Sir, this is not part of my questioning—"

"Is the death of Sextus's rival enough of a pattern?" Magnus continued.

Cicero pressed Fannius. "Sir, please direct the witness to answer only my questions."

"You broached the subject, Mr. Cicero," Fannius said.

"Sextus hated his brother just as he hated his father and they both ended up dead," Magnus said. "So, yes, I told my cousin of my uncle's murder, so he could look out for himself and not end up dead like the rest of our family."

Cicero hanged his head. All his work had just blown up in his face.

"Do you have further questions, Mr. Cicero?" Fannius asked.

"I…" Cicero's voice cracked. "I do not."

Cicero plodded back to his desk. As he passed, Erucius smiled patronizingly. "Qui bono?"

Chapter Ten

As the sun waned outside, Cicero sat with Caecillia at the table while Sextus stomped around their rickety tenement. Cicero was exhausted. He felt good about his opening statement and had punched holes in the stories of both witnesses. Maybe he had been over-confident, but as he pressed Magnus, Cicero could feel the momentum swaying his way. The crowd was already moving to his side, that much he was certain of, but Cicero could also see the doubt crossing the faces of the judges. Sextus had walked in there convicted in the minds of everyone, and Cicero had turned that all around. And he was doing it against one of the best lawyers in Rome. In a single moment, it all turned to ash.

"I don't understand. I didn't kill my brother or my father," Sextus said.

"Then why didn't you tell me about your brother's death?" Cicero asked.

"I didn't think about it. It was just an accident on the farm," Sextus said.

"Yes," Cicero said, "but if you had told me about it, I could have been prepared and spoken to the events. Instead, the judges saw claims of you killing another member of your family, and I was unable to refute them in any substantive manner. This is a disaster, Sextus."

Sextus crumbled into a seat, his head in his hands. Maybe Cicero had never swayed anyone to Sextus's side. Maybe the progress Cicero felt in the court was all in his head. Maybe he was headed toward a loss no matter what he did. Whatever the case, the doubt sowed by Magnus's insinuation that Sextus had murdered his brother was almost certainly the final blow.

"I'm sorry," Sextus said. "I—I don't know why I didn't say anything. I guess I knew how bad it all could look and I didn't want you to not believe me. You were the only one who would take the case. I—I...I'm so sorry."

Cicero sighed. He believed Sextus, but that didn't make their situation any better.

"So, what now?" Caecillia asked.

The room was silent.

"We can't just give up," Caecillia said.

"And I don't want to, but I don't know what else to do," Cicero said, thinking. After a moment, he looked at Sextus. "What exactly happened with your brother?"

"It was an accident," Sextus said.

"I believe you, I do," Cicero said. "But what exactly happened?"

"He was yoking an ox. Just got tangled in the harness and it trampled him," Sextus said. "But there was never, you know, a charge of murder. Swear it. If there was, the council of Ameria never would have fought these charges about my father's murder."

"Wait, what?" Cicero asked, perking up.

"There was never any charge or anything that I or anyone else killed my brother. It was an accident," Sextus said.

"Yes, but who were these people that spoke for you?" Cicero asked.

"The province leaders. The decuriones," Sextus said. "We were already in Rome when they did it, but they wrote a letter telling us that they had drafted an official petition of my innocence." Sextus let out a deep sigh. "And nothing came of it."

Cicero mulled on this a moment.

"And who did they petition?" Cicero asked.

"Sulla," Sextus said. "My father was a supporter of his, so we thought he would grant my pardon."

Cicero popped up and grabbed his things. "I have to go," he said. "If they filed that petition, then we could use it as evidence of their support of you."

Cicero stood in the entryway of Terentia's family's home, fidgeting. He was anxious to get to the records hall to search for the petition, but he was supposed to have dinner with Terentia and her family, so he had to make a quick stop. At least, he had hoped it would be quick. Instead, he'd been left to wait so long that he was considering leaving without even seeing Terentia.

Just then, Terentia turned the corner with one her handmaidens. Terentia and the woman argued a moment, but Terentia finally got her way and the other woman left the room. The odd moment had already concerned Cicero, but a pit formed in his stomach as Terentia approached and her red, irritated eyes became visible: she had been crying.

"What's wrong?" Cicero asked.

"You have to leave," Terentia said.

"I have to go to the hall of records. I'm sorry, but your handmaiden wasn't supposed to tell you," Cicero said.

"She didn't," Terentia said.

"Then why are you crying?" Cicero asked.

"My father said you have to go," Terentia asked. "He won't let us marry. Not if you continue with this trial. He said it's an embarrassment for the family."

"I know this is difficult to swallow, but it will be a feather in my cap and help me get new cases. Pretty soon, I might even be known enough to stand for office someday," Cicero said.

"That's what I told him," Terentia said. "He said it's hopeless. You'll never go anywhere with Sulla and Catiline against you, and he won't bring that shame into the family."

Cicero wanted to tell Terentia that it would all be fine. He wanted to tell her that he was going to win the case and that her father would eventually come around. He wanted to tell her all that and more. But he didn't want to lie.

Clouds of flickering candlelight filled in tiny portions of a voluminous and otherwise completely dark records hall. The space was empty except for Cicero, who dug through piles of documents.

Finishing one pile and moving it to the collection of others he had already perused, Cicero started on a fresh stack. The process had lasted hours, which had been a welcome distraction from his conversation with Terentia and his overall crumbling life. Moving swiftly through the current collection of documents, Cicero completed the pile and pushed it aside as he paused to rest his eyes. Exhausted, he dropped into a quick slumber with his elbow resting on the edge of the table. As he fell deeper into sleep, his elbow slipped under his weight, causing Cicero to tumble to the ground. In a fright, Cicero braced himself and gathered his wits again. As he rose he paused because a marking on a shelf of documents at the bottom of the shelves caught his eye: Ameria.

Cicero gathered the contents of the shelf in his arms and sifted through them. Halfway done, he paused and focused on one document. Cicero's face glowed with discovery. He tucked the document into his satchel and filed the rest of the papers back into the shelves.

With a newfound energy, Cicero grabbed his candle and scurried around the corner, then he stopped dead in his tracks as a boulder of a man turned the corner and glowered at him, his face scarred and weathered. Cicero heard another man approach from behind. He gulped.

Cicero stood alone in a cavernous but impeccably adorned library. Looking around the vast space, it seemed hard to believe that one man could have the resources to live in such luxury, but then again, this was not the library of just any man. Cicero was alone in the room, but candles in the hall projected the shapes of the stout guards just outside. Hearing approaching footsteps, Cicero's anxiety grew. He knew the cadence of these footfalls well.

From the hall a new shadow entered the room, preceding a familiar figure: Sulla. Sulla saw Cicero and smiled, warm and genuine, putting Cicero at immediate ease.

"Hello, Cicero."

"Hello, sir."

"It would seem you've gotten yourself into a spot of trouble."

"Just doing my job, sir."

"And it appears your job is to be a thorn in my side."

Cicero gulped.

"Relax," Sulla said. "You're safe here. I mean you no ill. On the contrary, I wish to offer you a job."

"A job, sir?"

"Yes. You will resign from your current trial and you will become a military tribune for me."

Cicero was taken aback. "Sir?"

"Is that not enough?" Sulla said. "It's better than what I offered you before, and it puts you in line to start the cursus honorum when you complete your term in the office. If I remember correctly, politics are your aim."

"Yes, sir. But…I left your service."

"Yes, you did."

"So, why would you want to help me?"

"I'm not. I'm asking you to help me. This trial is an embarrassment," Sulla said. "The system's been corrupted and one of my men has clearly done it."

"Catiline."

Sulla nodded. "Your old friend."

"So, you've known this whole time?" Cicero asked, confused.

"No, but you stirred up a hornet's nest with your arguments yesterday and gossip travels quickly," Sulla said.

"Then, step in. You can still save Sextus," Cicero said.

"I can't intervene. It would make a mockery of our justice system," Sulla said, looking around at his many law scrolls. Most of the ones Cicero could see had been barely if ever used. "But I also can't very well let there be the appearance of corruption within my ranks either."

"So what are you asking?" Cicero said.

"Quit the trial," Sulla said.

Cicero's gut tightened. He felt instantly sick, but as Sulla looked at him, Cicero knew he had to respond and it was not going to be what Sulla wanted to hear. Cicero steeled himself and took a breath. "I'm sorry, sir, but I have a responsibility to my client," Cicero said. "And to the law. Besides, sir, our differences have not been resolved."

"I know you don't respect the power I've taken, but look what I've done," Sulla said. "The Senate was so mired in in-fighting, posturing, and political maneuvering that nothing got done. I've changed that. I have the power to force change and reform. I want to reinforce the structure of the republic so that nobody can do what I've done, and I want you to help with that."

Cicero was stunned. This was what he'd always wanted. He could work to stabilize and build up the republic and he could do so from the inside, all while he built his own political career. It was perfect. It was everything he wanted. There was only one possible answer.

"No," Cicero said.

Sulla coughed out a stunned, incredulous laugh. "So, is this another grand display of your displeasure with my actions?"

"No, sir. It's just against my ethics," Cicero said.

"Your ethics?" Sulla said in a condescending tone.

Cicero gulped. "Yes, sir," he said. "Sextus Roscius is my client. It would go against my ethics as a lawyer and a Roman citizen to turn against him for personal gain."

"So, you think me an unethical man?" Sulla asked.

"No, sir," Cicero said, knowing his place. "We just have… different ethics."

Sulla cracked a smile. "Indeed you are a talented lawyer," he said. "Consider my offer, son. Your client will likely be found guilty either way, but if you walk away, I'll commute his sentence when things calm down and make sure no harm comes to him."

"But what about the next person who is unjustly charged, sir?" Cicero asked. "You can't step in after the fact with all of them. The system needs to work for everyone, not just people with powerful friends."

"I agree. And you can work on that in my administration," Sulla said. "I'm going to pretend you never told me no, because I want you to consider it further and think about the good you can do." Sulla motioned Cicero to the door. "Come on, I'll walk you out."

As they walked, Sulla looked to Cicero. "I understand you've been courting a young woman, Terentia Varrones," Sulla said.

Cicero stared back, confused. "Uh, yes sir."

"I had my people ask around about you when I heard about the trial," Sulla said. "I make sure to know everything about everything that impacts me. I actually know Terentia's father. He'd be lucky to have you as a son-in-law," Sulla said.

"I'm not sure he would agree with your assessment, sir," Cicero said.

"Well, marriage is the only thing more difficult to navigate than politics," Sulla said as they reached the door. "I'll expect your answer tomorrow, Cicero." Sulla paused, considering. "I hope you realize that everything I've done, I've done for Rome. And I know you are a man of the same ilk, Cicero. But you're also a gadfly. You have it in you to lead the republic. The only question is if you'll be drinking hemlock before you can do so."

Returning home, Cicero didn't bother crawling into bed. Instead, he sat in his apartment looking at a flickering oil lamp as his mind wandered. Sulla had indeed shown himself to be a reformer and he'd done much to help fix a broken system, but he came by his power unjustly. There could be no republic if powerful men took their posts without being placed in them by the will of the people. But for all his misgivings, Cicero knew he could also do much good under the umbrella of Sulla's unfettered power. In fact, with such power backing him, Cicero could institute all manner of governmental reforms with relative ease.

Cicero looked past the oil lamp to his father splayed out on the bed with one leg still on the floor and an arm cradling a jug of wine. Cicero had hoped that his father would rally and find cause to improve his situation with Cicero taking on such a high-profile case. But Tullius had simply carried on with his daily drinking rituals. Perhaps if Cicero wasn't so busy scrambling for work as a lawyer, he could help his father sober up. He could even give his father meaningful work and a reason to live again. With a post under the powerful Sulla, Cicero might even be able to get in the good graces of Terentia's father. That would certainly make life easier. Cicero went on like this for hours, his mind jumping from thought to thought, weighing the positives and negatives of each choice.

Finally, Cicero unfurled a blank scroll and readied his quill. Looking outside, he felt the city coming to life. He smiled and began to write, realizing he'd known the answer to his decision all along.

The next morning Sulla sat in his study, going over the paperwork piled upon his desk. He yawned and, for a moment, questioned his desire to be in charge at all. How much nicer life would be with enough sleep and time to spend with friends and family! As he did every morning, he shook off the thought and continued working.

A courier entered with a scroll. Sulla kept working as the courier set the scroll on his desk and went to leave without a word.

"One moment," Sulla said, and he finished signing his current document, then set it aside to unfurl the scroll and read.

Dictator Sulla,
    Respectfully, I must follow my own ethics.
—*Cicero*

Sulla smirked. He'd expected no less. Sulla set Cicero's scroll aside and pulled out a blank one. He looked to the courier. "I'll need this delivered straight away."

Leaving early, Cicero hit the streets before the sun bothered to show up for work. Sleep never happened, so why not get a jump on the day, he thought to himself, as he skipped along the cobblestone walkway. It had been a difficult night, but the past weeks and months had been difficult too, so Cicero didn't feel the strain he might have if things had been going well. In fact, he felt pretty good. He'd suspected Catiline had rigged the trial against his client, but now he knew for certain and there was liberation in the certainty. He was free to argue the case with impunity. He truly had nothing left to lose, but his client had much to lose and Cicero was going to give Sextus the best chance for acquittal he could.

After writing his note to Sulla early this morning, Cicero pulled out a scroll and wrote his closing argument. A masterful record keeper, Cicero wrote out all his arguments and stored them away, including the one with which he had opened this particular trial. But in writing his closing argument this time,

Cicero had a unique experience. Usually, writing was a tortured experience for him, filled with stops, starts, and frequent rewrites. His active mind often worked against his quill, finding the flaws in his work before he'd finished composing it, necessitating the reworking of the entire document. This time, however, Cicero knew everything before he put it down. Not once did he walk back his thoughts or change direction. He wrote what his mind dictated and never looked back. Free from his own expectations for success, Cicero was finally able to focus his mind on nothing but the matter at hand. Would it win the case? Not likely, but Cicero certainly enjoyed the ease of the experience.

Cresting the final hill, Cicero saw the Forum ahead. He stopped and took a moment to enjoy the warm sun creeping over the hills. If nothing else, he had given the trial his all. It might not do much for his career, but at least he had done his duty and would be able to sleep at night. That is, as soon as he stopped worrying enough to start sleeping again.

Approaching the Forum, Cicero slowed to find the area filled with people. What's going on? Is there an election today? Coming to the Forum this early usually meant one's only companions were pigeons and the drunks stumbling past on their way home. Actually, regardless of the time of day, Cicero had never seen so many people crammed into the Forum at *any* time.

"Excuse me," Cicero said approaching an old plebeian woman. "Is there some event happening?"

The old woman looked on Cicero with a matter-of-fact nod. "Sure is. Trial of century they're calling it. Only wish I'd come yesterday."

Cicero paused, confused. How had he not heard about this trial yet? Was he so consumed by his own travails that he'd not even heard the chatter about this massive trial?

"Eh, hey…right there. That's him," a snaggletooth plebe hollered to a friend, as he pointed behind Cicero.

Cicero turned, but there was no one there. Looking back, he realized the plebe was pointing at *him*. Cicero's stomach dropped.

"Yep, that be him fer sure," the plebe continued. "Cicero. That's what they be calling him." The plebe marched over to pat Cicero on the shoulder and shake his unoffered hand. "Real fine to meet you, sir. Real fine."

Cicero couldn't help but chuckle. A stranger had never known who he was, nor had there ever been a reason for someone to know him by reputation. It was also odd to be referred to as "sir" by someone who certainly doubled him in age, but Cicero had no time to dwell on such things as the crowd closed in around him.

Hands came from all angles, patting Cicero on the back as their owners shouted out encouragements: "Atta boy"…"you show 'em"…"give 'em hell." But soon the crowd grew uncomfortably dense around Cicero. The attention, at first gratifying, grew frightening.

"Thank you, thank you. I need to get to the court, but thank you," Cicero said, trying to weave his way through as people kept moving in toward him. Despite their well-wishes, Cicero grew uncomfortable, finding no way out of the crowd.

"All right, that's enough. Out of the way," a voice said from out of Cicero's view. Finally, the crowd parted and Cicero smiled to see an old friend: Gaius Julius Caesar. "Come on," Caesar said to Cicero, "Let's get you in there."

∼

Caesar and Cicero entered the courtyard to find it empty of the people crowding around outside but still filled with their noise. Cicero had thought that the area was large when it was filled yesterday, but without the gallery it seemed twice the size. The space was clean and the tables and seating were already set up for the end of the trial, but Cicero and Caesar choose to sit at the back of a row set up for the spectators.

"Hell of a spectacle you've created," Caesar said with a smirk.

"What have I gotten myself into?" Cicero said.

"Not sure what you're into, but whatever it is, you're in up to your eyes," Caesar said.

Cicero sighed and smiled to his friend. "Regardless, it is nice to see you again. Why are you here?"

Caesar looked on Cicero, bemused. "Don't you know? Like everyone else, I'm here for the trial."

"Why?" Cicero asked.

"Everyone is talking about it, my friend," Caesar said. "For a soft-spoken guy, you sure know how to speak up. It's amazing you've lived this long, going against Sulla twice now. Can't imagine you're his favorite person these days."

"I saw him yesterday," Cicero said.

"What? When?" Caesar asked, stunned. "What did he say?"

Cicero shrugged. "He offered to name me military tribune and sponsor me for the cursus honorum."

Stunned, Caesar stared back. Caesar was an ambitious man—more than any Cicero knew. On more than one occasion, Caesar had to set aside his morals to make way for his ambition. Caesar hadn't agreed with Sulla's actions in taking control of Rome any more than Cicero had, but he set those feelings aside to stay in the good graces of the great man. Yet, here was

Cicero being offered the opportunity of a lifetime from a man he had twice scorned. It made Caesar very angry, not so much with Cicero but with himself.

Caesar had always liked Cicero and respected him as a man of honor, but even treasured friendships could be filled with the rivalry of siblings. Caesar wasn't as smart as Cicero, but he knew himself to be ten times the solider and at least equal the politician. Of course, it was hard to argue he was the political equal of a man if he was so routinely overlooked in favor of him.

"What did he want?" Caesar asked.

Cicero looked down, almost ashamed. "For me to quit."

Caesar nodded. Well, perhaps Cicero wasn't such a man of honor after all.

"Have you told your client yet?" Caesar asked.

"I'm not quitting. I told Sulla no," Cicero said.

"What? Why?" Caesar asked.

"It would be against my ethics to turn my back on my client like that. Besides, he's innocent of the charges," Cicero said.

Caesar looked at Cicero again, this time with none of the jealousy that he had felt before. Cicero may have gotten some chances that Caesar had not, but clearly this was a man who could not get out of his own way.

"You're mad," Caesar said.

"So it would seem," Cicero said.

"Well, I'll let you get to your preparations," Caesar said. "You give them your best and maybe you'll get out of this alive."

Cicero paused. Sure, he had considered the danger in going up against powerful people like this, but hearing it from the mouth of another was a different experience altogether. Nonetheless, he had an argument to give today and he could not let such thoughts cloud his thinking.

"I know this must all seem terribly unwise," Cicero said. "But I have to do this. Besides, I do not believe Sulla to be a man who will do something as tawdry as kill a lawyer for arguing a case."

"I wasn't talking about Sulla," Caesar said, cocking an eyebrow and nodding to the back of the courtyard where a tall, well-heeled man stood, his intense, cold eyes fixed on Cicero. It was Catiline.

"Looks like you're going to have quite an audience today," Caesar said, patting Cicero on the back before walking away.

"Patricide," Erucius said, pacing before the judges. "That is the charge we are all here to examine. The cold-blooded murder of a father by his son. The defense can pretend that Sextus Roscius the Younger did not kill his father, and they can come up with all manner of outlandish explanations as to who actually did, but that which is not true is not true no matter how hard one tries to contort and manipulate the falsity to fit into the shape of truth."

Cicero looked at Erucius as the litigator argued his case. Erucius was Cicero's combatant in this case, but Cicero could not help but appreciate the ease with which Erucius stated his case. He spoke with such gravitas and weight but did so in a natural, engaging voice. It was not a lecture and it was not conversation, but something else. Something so consuming that even though Cicero knew Erucius's words were demonstrably false, he could not help but be taken with them on an emotional level.

Cicero felt comfortable with his arguments overall, but he knew he lacked the style that Erucius brought. Cicero's words carried formidable substance, but he knew they were not worth as much as Erucius's because he did not speak them in an oratorical style that could sway an undecided mind. For Sextus's sake,

Cicero hoped the deep substance of his words would be enough to carry the day.

"Qui bono? Who benefits?" Erucius continued. "That is the cornerstone of the defense's weak, faltering case." Erucius paused, glowering at Cicero for all to see like a disappointed father. "Make no mistake though," he continued, "for as impotent as his case may be, Mr. Cicero is a man of great intelligence and wile. Unfortunately for him, he has no evidence to support his client's claims of innocence, so he's been forced to angle all his intellectual might toward manufacturing a false narrative aimed at casting doubt on his client's guilt, and it all teeters on the simple argument that his client did not benefit from his father's death. But it is that very argument that buries his client."

Cicero looked on with apprehension, not certain where Erucius was going.

"You see," Erucius said, "if we are seeking only those who benefitted from the death of Sextus Roscius the Elder, there is but one direction to look."

Erucius stepped to the center of the courtyard and, in a grand performance, he posed, dramatically stretching his arm to point to the defense table.

"Sextus...Roscius...the Younger," Erucius called out with all the weight of his strident voice. Erucius held his stare, as the courtroom fell silent.

"Because, you see," Erucius continued, "if not for us all being here today for this very trial, Sextus Roscius the Younger, that very man over there...he would have benefitted from his father's most untimely of deaths. With his older brother dead, the brother that was first in line to receive their father's vast land holdings, Sextus stood to receive everything. And I can regale you with all the tawdry details of his brother's mysterious death from just a year ago, but we're not here to send Mr. Roscius to his death for his brother's murder. No, we're here because he murdered his *father*."

"So, yes, I agree with Mr. Cicero," Erucius said. "Qui bono is at the heart of this case, and the only way to keep the perpetrator of this heinous act from benefitting from it is to find him guilty of the crime we already know he committed."

Erucius stopped and looked at the judges dramatically.

"So, our fine judges," Erucius said, putting weight on each word. "I humbly ask each of you to consider all you have gleaned from of these arguments and order the death of the only man who could have benefitted from the murder of Sextus Roscius the Elder."

Erucius turned to the crowd: "His son."

Erucius waited a moment, playing up the drama with the flair of a master actor, then finally relented and stepped back to his table. As he passed, Erucius offered Cicero a snide smile.

Cicero took in a deep breath, feeling the stares of what felt like the entirety of the world turning toward him. He looked down at his shaking hands. At once, he felt all the heat of the early day's sun radiating upon him. He took in a breath but couldn't seem to get enough air. He tried to remember his argument, but nothing came to mind.

Sextus and Caecillia looked at each other with concern. Murmurs built within the crowd. Finally, Praetor Fannius cleared his throat. "Mr. Cicero, are you prepared to give your closing argument?"

Cicero could not remember a thing he'd written. Feeling the stares of the audience, Cicero looked around the room, his gaze inevitably turning to Catiline in the back of the room. The pressure was too much—

A hand slipped onto Cicero's shoulder. He turned to see his father and Terentia seated behind him. Cicero had not even introduced his father to Terentia and yet, there they were together. And his father was sober. Cicero could not help but crack a small smile. But as he smiled, Terentia nodded to the proceedings before him. Cicero sat to attention, at once remembering everything. Then he stood.

"I'm sorry, Praetor," Cicero said. "I am prepared to give my final argument." He closed his eyes just a moment and gathered himself. Finally, he opened his eyes, ready.

"Thank you all for your patience," Cicero said looking from the praetor to the judges to the crowd. "And thank you for coming into this trial with an open mind. It's a difficult charge, patricide. The most serious a citizen of Rome can be accused of. And that is exactly why we must examine every facet of it. And why we must look at all possible perpetrators and not just assume that the man accused is the guilty party.

"Now, we've just heard from Erucius. He is a master orator. That is without question. There is perhaps no man in Rome more capable of arguing a case. I know I am not his equal. And yet, for all his ability, it must be noted that there is little substance to the words he just spoke. You see, while he is my better in style, I have the benefit of something so powerful that not even the most eloquent man in Rome can defeat it," Cicero said, turning to look at Erucius, "the truth."

"The problem with truth is that no amount of power can change it and no amount of effort can obscure it," Cicero said. "Not completely. What is true is true, even when attacked by a man of incredible influence and political might. A man like…"

Cicero turned and pointed unambiguously at Catiline, his motion causing the crowd to part to view the subject of Cicero's motion.

"Lucius Sergius Catilina. Catiline. The second man to Dictator Sulla. One of the great powers of Rome. But we'll come back to Catiline," Cicero said.

"First, I want to talk to you all about Sextus Roscius the Younger, the defendant. This is a man who loved and respected his father, and he loved his life in Ameria. The prosecution can say all they want that he hated his father and hated Ameria, but again, the truth gets in their way. Sextus never wished to live in Rome like his father, because he truly loves Ameria and its people. As proof, I wish to present the court this."

Cicero pulled from his satchel a scroll, unspooling and setting it before Erucius. "Mr. Erucius, since I assume you have yet to see this, can you please tell the court what this is?" he asked.

Erucius glowered at Cicero but did not deign to glance at the document held before him.

"I'm sorry, Erucius," Cicero said, "are you not interested in looking at a piece of evidence? Are you not interested in…the truth?" Cicero picked up the scroll. "It's fine. I'll tell everyone for you."

Cicero held the scroll up high for all to see. "This is a petition that was signed by all the leaders of Ameria, pleading for Sulla to step in and stop the accusations of patricide against my client, Sextus Roscius the Younger."

Cicero stepped to the judges, walking along them with the petition outstretched. "As a cornerstone of their community, which the prosecution would have you believe he hates, the people of Ameria came together to speak for one of their local sons.

Hardly seems like a person who was forced to live there would be so universally loved by the rest of the residents, does it?"

"Give it here, Mr. Cicero," Praetor Fannius said, as Cicero handed it over. Fannius scanned over the document, then nodded. "This is legitimate," Fannius said to the judges. "You may consider this as evidence for the accused."

"Thank you, Praetor," Cicero said. When Fannius handed the document back, Cicero stopped him. "Actually, before you give that back, your honor, will you please read who signed the receipt of this document that was meant for Dictator Sulla?"

Fannius looked at Cicero with annoyance, but relented. As he read, he paused. Finally, taking a breath and he said, "Lucius Sergius Catiline."

"Catiline," Cicero said to the gallery with faux amazement. "Now, that is interesting."

Erucius stood, bellowing out to the court, "This is outrageous. Of course Mr. Catiline would receive such a document. As an officer of the republic, it is his job. If Mr. Cicero is going to call out one of the great citizens of Rome, he should do so for something more damning than that the man was performing a task of his job."

"Of course. Yes. You are correct, Erucius." Cicero again went to take the document, but again stopped. "Actually, Praetor, will you read one more part for us?"

Fannius was not pleased with being used as a prop but looked back at the document anyway.

"Thank you, Praetor," Cicero said. "Can you tell us all the name of the citizen who delivered this document?"

Fannius scanned the document and started to speak, but stopped, stunned. Finally, he mouthed something quietly.

"I'm sorry, but can you say that for everyone to hear?" Cicero asked.

Fannius sighed and projected to the crowd, gravely serious, "Capito Roscius."

The courtyard let out a collective gasp that quickly dissolved to deafening chatter, as everyone from the judges to the gallery mulled over the revelation. Erucius stood, trying to yell through the noise, to no avail. In the back, Catiline looked at the chaos with apprehension, as Capito and Magnus slumped down in their seats in the first row.

Finally, Praetor Fannius stood and waved the crowd quiet, barely making the headway necessary to have his voice heard. "Silence! I will have silence or I will have this courtyard cleared," Fannius hollered, his voice straining to carry though the din.

With the clamor finally dying down, Erucius again projected his previously drowned-out words. "This is nonsense. That is merely a case of a family member trying to help another family member."

As boos flew at Erucius from audience, Cicero stepped forward, waving down the riled spectators.

"Hold your emotions, my friends. We must keep our decorum," Cicero said to the quieting crowd. "I am shocked by the information too, but we can't lose sight of what this revelation means. Because if it is true that Capito was just trying to help his cousin free himself from the burdens of the awful accusations against him, then the testimony Capito and Magnus gave to us yesterday about knowing Sextus wanted his father dead must not be true."

Cicero turned to Erucius. "So, which is it? Did Capito believe his cousin was innocent and struck out to defend him from the charges, or had he and Magnus suspected him immediately in the death of his father, as they testified?" Cicero waited on Erucius to answer. Erucius stared coldly back but did not speak.

Cicero turned to the judges. "This is where the lie begins to unravel," he said. "Because Capito and Magnus both testified that even before the murder of their uncle, they suspected Sextus of harboring ill will for his father. If that is the case, why would Capito then not just sign but stand as representative for a document pleading for the charges against Sextus to be canceled?"

Cicero looked on Erucius a moment, as if waiting for an answer. "It would appear as though Erucius has no explanation for this. I suspect that is so because there is only one answer and it is that Capito took the petition not because he sought to save his cousin and make sure it got to Sulla, but because he wanted to make sure it did *not*. Instead, he took it straight to the cohort he and Magnus had been in league with all along: Catiline."

"This is madness," Erucius said, bolting from his chair. "Catiline is a respected citizen of Rome and one of its most powerful administrators. If he did not believe in the innocence of Sextus Roscius then that is why he did not cancel the charges against him."

"Or was it because he was the one who brought the charges against Sextus to begin with?" Cicero asked. "That seems to me like a definite conflict of interest. Perhaps such a respected citizen should have avoided the conflict and given the petition to the man to whom it was addressed."

"Catiline's supposed dereliction of duty is hardly an offense that can absolve Sextus Roscius of his crime against his father," Erucius said.

"No, but conspiracy is," Cicero barked back at Erucius, waiting a moment for his words to sink in with the crowd.

Finally, Cicero looked to the judges, speaking with a calm, exacting demeanor. "After the death of Sextus's older brother, which was simply a farm accident and was never considered murder, or the leaders of Ameria would never have come out in support of Sextus now. But again, after the death of Sextus's older bother, I submit that Capito and Magnus conspired to murder their uncle and blame it on Sextus. With the older brother out of the way, there was just a single heir remaining between them and their uncle's land, so they were clear to commit the crime and hang it around the neck of the naïve younger brother: my client, Sextus Roscius the Younger."

"The conspiracy was simple," Cicero continued. "Magnus, the former gladiator would do the killing, Capito, the local farmhand, would handle the townspeople, and Catiline, the ruthless powerbroker, would make sure Roscius was convicted."

Erucius stood, clapping mockingly as he rolled his eyes. "And what a conspiracy Mr. Cicero has dreamed up in his head," Erucius said, looking from the crowd to the judges. "But that is all it is. Just an idea in Mr. Cicero's head, because outside of a simple document that proves nothing, he has no evidence of his claims, and he certainly has no evidence to show why a powerful man such at Catiline would even bother with such an insane venture."

"How about greed?" Cicero retorted. "Would that motivate a man to conspire against another?"

"More baseless claims," Erucius laughed.

"Claims, yes. But they are not without base," Cicero said, pulling another document from his satchel. "Here, I have a deed of sale for the land, which, prior to the accusations leveled against him, was to be Sextus Roscius the Younger's."

Cicero handed the document to Fannius. Fannius looked it over, growing paler by the moment. Reluctantly, he nodded. "This is genuine."

Cicero took back the document. "Thank you, Praetor, I will not ask you to read the name this time. I will do that," Cicero said, turning to the audience. "This is a deed from the sale of ten farms from Sextus Roscius the Elder's estate, and it is written out to the new owner, Lucius Sergius Catilina."

Anticipating another reaction from the crowd, Erucius jumped to his feet before Cicero could finish reading. "This is nothing," he barked. "Catiline has the right to buy property like any other citizen."

"Indeed he does," Cicero said. "But this deed does return us to what I have argued all along would point to the true perpetrator of this crime. Qui bono? Who benefits? And now we know that it is Catiline."

"Buying property and inheriting it are two very different things," Erucius said. "It is a poor criminal who kills someone for something, only to pay for it anyway."

"That is true," Cicero conceded. "Catiline did buy the property at auction—a vast estate that was valued at more than three million sesterces. And he bought it all for…" Cicero handed the praetor the form. "I'm sorry, your honor, but I will require your services once more."

Fannius looked over the paper, then looked up to see the stern eyes of a fuming Catiline piercing through him. Fannius took a breath. "Two thousand sesterces."

Gasps poured in from the crowd.

"I'm sorry, sir," Cicero said. "Can you say that again?"

"Two thousand sesterces," Fannius said.

Cicero turned and stepped to the middle of the courtyard. "Two thousand sesterces for ten farms valued at three million sesterces."

"You said yourself it was a public auction. The price was not set," Erucius said.

"That is true," Cicero said. "And I'm sure Catiline did not bring any soldier or armed guards with him to make sure he got such an incredible price." Cicero laughed to himself, as he looked from the crowd to the judges. "Qui bono."

Cicero took a moment to look upon the sea of gazing faces within the gallery of spectators. He peered over at Magnus and Capito, both looking more ill than angered. He smiled to see his father and Terentia. He saw the look of hope in the eyes of Sextus and Caecillia for the first time since he'd known them. Finally, he looked at Catiline and saw nothing but the anger and the selfishness of the kind of man who would burn the entire republic down just for personal gain.

"Qui bono," Cicero said again. "Who benefitted from the death of Sextus Roscius the Elder? Catiline? He owns a vast estate that he bought for almost nothing. Magnus Roscius? He now owns three of his uncle's farms, gifted to him by Catiline. Capito Roscius? Once a poor farmhand, he now serves as caretaker to all of the properties. Or was it Sextus Roscius the Younger, the son of the deceased? He no longer lives in his beloved Ameria. He owns no farms. He gained nothing and yet he sits accused."

Erucius looked on, ready for the day to end.

"But, as I'm sure you are all thinking, Erucius told us that if not for their actions in bringing Sextus to trial, he would have been the sole beneficiary of his father's death. And that is true. And coming from such a well-respected lawyer, it is hard to take those words lightly. But regardless of his words, his case is so slight, so lacking in evidence that if not for Erucius's incredible rhetorical talents, there would be no case at all. And that made me wonder why Erucius would take it in the first place."

Erucius sat to attention, suddenly filled with a nervous energy the calm and cool litigator had not shown thus far.

"Why would such an esteemed litigator as Erucius take on something so unworthy of his talents?" Cicero continued. "In uncovering the documents I shared with you today, I encountered one that answered my question."

Cicero reached in his satchel once more, pulling out a last document. Holding it up to the crowd, then the judges, Cicero finally handed it to Praetor Fannius, as he looked back to the courtyard filled with people.

"You see, in looking over the ownership records, I saw that Catiline bought ten properties, but after he gave three to Magnus, he ended up with just six of the original farms. After some digging, I found the owner of the one missing farm: Erucius," Cicero said, almost disappointed to have to buried such a worthy adversary. "A gift, it would seem, from his fellow conspirators."

Erucius looked to Fannius, who gave just a single, disgusted shake of his head.

Cicero looked to a crowd that was too stunned to even boo this time. "It would seem that the only person that did not benefit from this murder is the defendant."

With the crowd paying rapt attention, Cicero walked along the judges, looking on each in silence.

"My fellow Romans," Cicero said, "Sextus Roscius the Younger is innocent of these accusations. He was a good son, who loved his father and loved his life, and because of greed, all that was taken from him. Who is responsible for the death of

Sextus Roscius the Elder? The answer is the same now as it has always been. Qui bono? Who benefitted?"

Cicero turned from the judges, silently pointing his finger first to Erucius, then Capito, Magnus, and finally Catiline. As Cicero held the accusing pose, Catiline stood and marched off with his bodyguards, never taking his scowling eyes off Cicero.

After the hearing ended and the judges stepped away to deliberate, Cicero intended to talk to Terentia, then sneak away to a quiet space with Sextus and Caecillia to await word on the verdict. However, as the judges walked off to decide Sextus's fate and Cicero went to pack his bag, swarms of onlookers descended upon him. So, instead of awaiting the results in quiet, Cicero found himself trading handshakes and receiving pats on the back. Such attention and adulation were new and strange phenomena to Cicero, but from the many well-wishers he had already received two dozen job offers, so it was all a welcome discomfort. After this, if Cicero could manage to not be killed by Catiline, he might actually be able to make a decent living at the law.

"I'm sorry," Cicero said, looking to Terentia. "I think they're almost done."

"No, this is good," Terentia said.

"This has to be a good sign, right?" Sextus said.

Cicero paused, then turned to the remaining people waiting to talk with him. "I need to talk with my client." Cicero looked to Terentia. "I want to talk with you, but just give me a moment with Sextus."

"Of course," Terentia said.

Cicero turned from the crowd and sat beside Sextus and Caecillia, his sober mood a stark contrast to the jubilant tone of the room.

"What's wrong?" Caecillia asked.

Cicero took a moment, organizing his thoughts. "The crowd is on our side. And that is certainly a good thing. But it may not matter for the verdict. You are being judged by the Senators of Rome. They are not as easily swayed as the average citizen."

At once, Cicero felt awful for basking in the attention of the crowd and not considering the situation fully. After a verdict was read, the sentence was immediately given and immediately carried out. These could be Sextus's last moments.

"But your argument was so good. You swayed them, I just know it," Caecillia said. Cicero saw that she truly believed her words, but Sextus finally understood that justice might not be done for him.

"They all know Catiline," Sextus said.

Cicero nodded and lowered his head. "He is an elite like them. I'm sure many, if not most, have dealt directly with him."

"But that could be in our favor, right?" Caecillia said. "He's not an honorable man. Surely he has done ill to them as well."

"Possibly, yes. But even then…" Cicero said, searching for the right sentiment. "Perhaps you should go, Sextus."

For charges of grave importance, the accused were often allowed to leave the city before the reading of the verdict and before the sentence was handed down. Such a luxury was usually afforded to the wealthy, but in this case Cicero suspected all involved would just be happy to have the situation resolve itself calmly.

"But how would that look?" Sextus said. "I'd seem as guilty as the ones that did it."

"But you'd be alive," Cicero said.

Just then, the curtains parted at the top of the stairs and Praetor Fannius entered, leading the judges back into the courtyard. Cicero's stomach dropped. He'd spent so much time basking in the adulation of the masses that he neglected to look after his client.

"Do we need to go?" Caecillia asked. "Should we leave?"

"It's too late," Sextus said.

Cicero sighed. "I'm so sorry, Sextus. I wasn't thinking and I—" Cicero stopped as Sextus put a hand to his arm and looked calmly in his eyes.

"You have nothing to be sorry about, Cicero," Sextus said. "You believed me when no one else would. If this is my last day, so be it. At least the truth came out and we have only you to thank for that."

Sextus's words, meant as a kindness, pierced Cicero like a rusty blade. However true the words were, Cicero could not shake the feeling that he had not done enough.

"Will the defendant please stand," Fannius said from the fore of the stairs. Sextus stood and Cicero stood with him.

"For the charges leveled against you by the esteemed Catiline and argued by the esteemed Erucius, the judges have rendered a verdict," Fannius said.

Cicero's palms dripped with nervous sweat and his mouth ran dry. He looked to Terentia, then Sextus and Caecillia. Caecillia was barely holding herself together, but Sextus was the picture of calm. Cicero peered around the courtyard. The area was once again filled but now with seemingly more people than ever. But amongst the sea of humanity, Catiline was nowhere to be seen. Cicero looked to the front to find both Capito and Magnus also absent. Finally, Cicero looked to Erucius. Once proud, bordering on arrogant, Erucius stared at the ground, a defeated man. He has been abandoned. Cicero knew the verdict before it was read.

"In a tally of 20 votes to none," Fannius projected to the crowd. "Sextus Roscius the Younger is found not guilty of patricide."

The crowd erupted into cheers. Sextus and Caecillia hugged and cried, breaking just long enough for Sextus to shake Cicero's hand. No words were traded between the two men, just silent, mutual gratitude.

Chapter Eleven

Cicero marched up the steps to his third-floor apartment. Exhausted from the trial, each step was a task, but he tried not to show it, as Terentia followed behind. Nonetheless, his mind wandered to a future where he could afford a bottom floor abode and not have to be sweaty and out of breath every time he walked into his home. Such may not be the case tomorrow, but after such a victory, he would certainly be able to afford to move within the year.

"Are you sure you don't wish to go back to celebrate? Everyone was so excited for you," Terentia said. Maybe it was the emotion of it all, but Cicero had to get out of there. Besides, he really just wished to spend time with Terentia. But now that he had the time to think of something other than his case, Cicero realized he did not know how Terentia had been allowed to attend the trial.

"What happened today?" Cicero asked.

"What do you mean?" Terentia asked.

"Your father…You said you couldn't see me anymore. He forbade it," Cicero said.

"He changed his mind," Terentia said. "I don't know what happened. A messenger showed up this morning with a letter, and after my father read it, he insisted I come today."

"A letter? From whom?" Cicero asked.

"It had Sulla's seal," Terentia said.

"Sulla?" Cicero said, confused. Had Sulla encouraged Terentia's father to approve of him as a suitor? Cicero had talked with Sulla about Terentia and her father, but he had not expected him to care, much less speak for him. Cicero and Sulla had always gotten along and, even though Cicero did not agree with the great man's methods, he had always respected Sulla as a man of deep substance and ability. Nonetheless, Cicero taking this case had been an incredible thorn in Sulla's side. Catiline was his ally, so not just going against his word as the accuser of Sextus but placing ample blame on him for the crime put Cicero directly at odds with Sulla. And yet Sulla had intervened to help him in a matter of love. It was almost too much to contemplate.

As they reach the top of the stairs, Cicero slowed and looked to Terentia.

"Whatever the reasoning, I am grateful your father changed his mind about me," Cicero said. "But you should know before we enter into my home that my father is not a well man. He took to wine heavily after my mother's death and..." Cicero thought for a moment. "He is not a well man, but he is still a good man, so do not judge him too harshly."

Terentia smiled, taking Cicero's hand in a reassuring grip. "He raised you, so of course he is a good man."

Cicero smiled and opened the door—

Cicero halted, immediately blocking Terentia from entering, as he saw four stout men waiting in his apartment.

"Who are you to come to my home like this?" Cicero asked with a strident confidence he had not known he possessed.

"Calm yourself, my friend," Caesar said, stepping out from Cicero's father's room.

"Caesar? What are you—"

"Congratulations on your victory," Caesar said. "Of course, I knew you had it in you. Nobody is more stubborn than Cicero, I said. Nobody believed me though, but here we are."

Cicero grew concerned. "You can kill me if you must," he said, "but leave Terentia be."

Caesar let out a hearty laugh. "Dear friend, I am not here to kill you. I am here to keep you safe."

"From whom?" Cicero asked.

"From the enemies you are in no short supply of these days," Caesar said. "You have a long journey, and they will certainly want to keep you from making it."

"Journey? What are you talking about?" Cicero said, relaxing a little but still not ready to trust the situation fully.

"You're being sent to Sicily," Caesar said. "Seems you've put Sulla in a bind. You are too liked to be killed, yet too hated to be kept safe in the city. Plus, he can't very well have a gadfly like you hovering around, openly challenging the men of his administration. Even those like Catiline."

"So, I'm to be exiled?" Cicero said.

"No, you are being rewarded," Caesar said. "Sulla is making you the assistant to the Quaestor of Sicily. And when his term is complete, you will take his place. Truly, it is a phenomenon I do not understand. It would seem the more you thumb your nose at the greatest man in Rome, the more he respects you."

Cicero had no words in retort. He'd given up all realistic hope of achieving a political career, and the trial, he had thought, would be the final word on such. And yet, here he was, being given that which he had sought all along. So why did it not feel right?

"And what if I say no?" Cicero asked.

Caesar shrugged. "I'm sorry, friend, but nobody is asking you."

Chapter Twelve

Cicero lifted a pear from a fruit vendor's wagon, felt its firm flesh, and knew immediately that it was not ripe, but he brought it to his nose out of habit nonetheless. Its lack of scent confirmed his suspicions.

"No, no, Sir Cicero. Is not good," the fruit vendor said, using just enough broken Latin to be understood through his Sicilian accent. "This," the vendor said, handing Cicero another pear. "Much gooder. Much."

Cicero smiled and reached for his coin purse.

"No, no. No pay. Free to Sir Cicero," the vendor said.

"Thank you, Septimius," Cicero said, handing over payment. Each day they had the same exchange and each day Cicero left money anyway. While flattering to have the respect of the vendor, Cicero could never betray the man's kindness by taking him up on his offer.

As much as Cicero enjoyed this routine exchange with his favorite fruit seller, such experiences were becoming increasingly common. While certainly not a hardship, Cicero found it all a little awkward. Cicero did not want to offend someone by not respecting an offer, but he had grown rich these past years, so it would be wrong not to pay for goods from people far less fortunate. Did Caius Verres ever enjoy such encounters with his subjects? Cicero doubted it.

Cicero's time in Sicily started quietly. Apprenticing under the quaestor of the time, Cicero had learned much about public administration within the republic and even more about the accounting of public monies. The latter, however, made his current time in Sicily much less quiet.

Walking through the town square, Cicero approached an open area and sat in his usual seat. Perched upon the rocks overlooking the sea, Cicero breathed in the crisp air and admired the view. While he thought of Rome on most days, living in Syracuse had been a blessing. The capital of the province, Syracuse was a city of Greek origin and one Cicero had come to believe was the most beautiful of the Hellenistic world.

After successfully defending Sextus Roscius, Cicero was forced to leave Rome for his own safety, but more so for the safety of Sulla's administration. Despite the pressure Cicero was able to talk his way into staying long enough to marry Terentia, but it was a rushed affair and soon he found himself taking his bride on a honeymoon of an indeterminate length.

Cicero did not marry Terentia for her family's money, but such certainly came in handy as they began life together in exile. Though Cicero had little choice in leaving, Sulla had not hung him out to dry. Instead, Sulla set up Cicero with a post that would allow him to learn public administration in preparation for a quaestorship, the first slot in cursus honorum. Unfortunately, at the time of his expulsion from the city, Cicero's promised job would not be open for almost a year, so he and Terentia had to find somewhere to spend their time.

First, they set sail for Asia Minor, then Rhodes, and finally Greece. Terentia had her misgivings about leaving Rome, given it was the only place she'd ever lived, but travel agreed with her and she and Cicero grew close. But, as much as their travels served as a honeymoon, ever the pragmatist, Cicero used it as an opportunity to better his skills.

During the trial of Sextus Roscius, Cicero found great reason to be confident in the substance of his arguments. But in seeing Erucius's masterful presentations, Cicero knew he had much to learn rhetorically. So, while Terentia wandered through markets or enjoyed the warm waters of the Aegean, Cicero would steal away to learn from the greatest oratory instructors of the day: the Greeks.

Cicero also studied composition and learned to hone his legal arguments in writing. In starting his legal career, Cicero always took great care to put his thoughts and legal arguments in writing. This proved a fortuitous exercise, as after his successful defense of Sextus Roscius, a great many lawyers approached Cicero, looking to read his material for the case. Cicero obliged them, hiring a scribe to transcribe the writings. The subsequent works he released under the title of *In Defense of Roscius Ameria*. Since then, he made quite a sum reading from his work and offering advice and instruction to new lawyers.

Cicero took a long look at the sea. Rome may have been the center of the world, but it failed to achieve the simple beauty of the area outstretched before him. Regardless, Cicero longed to return to his home. Fresh air and beauty provided simple joy, but he couldn't help but miss Rome's cramped streets and unpleasant but familiar odors.

Cicero lifted his satchel to the tabletop and pulled from it a thick packet of papers. Beside the packet, he set a quill and blank scroll. At the beginning of his exile, letter writing was more of a discipline and a duty meant to keep him in touch with the political world he had left behind, but in recent times it had become more of an emotional need. Since his father's death, Cicero leaned deeper into his friendships back in Rome, as he had no living family remaining. Receiving a letter from an old friend made him feel at ease and connected to the world. In a cruel twist of fate, the better life became for Cicero both professionally and intellectually, the more strain fell on his personal life.

Initially, his father was to travel from Rome with him and Terentia, but when the time came to leave, Tullius disappeared. Cicero never found out the reasons for his father's disappearance, but he suspected Tullius just could not leave behind the world he had shared with Helvia. Cicero received a few letters from his father, but those stopped in time. He heard from others that Tullius fell harder into drink, but even those reports started to dry up and nothing was heard of Tullius for nearly a year. Then, after months of nothing, Cicero received word of his father's death. It hit Cicero hard, losing his father, but he tried to assuage the pain with the thought that maybe his father had found the peace in death that he was lacking in life. Hopefully, Tullius and Helvia were together again somewhere. Nonetheless, Cicero's struggles with his father's death only got worse when things began to sour with Terentia.

Being so far from her friends and family was difficult for Terentia initially, but as newlyweds she and Cicero grew closer and such concerns faded. For the first few years of their marriage, life was easy. Cicero and Terentia basked in their discovery of each other and the world around them. As they traveled across Greece and Asia Minor, they grew closer. When Cicero and Terentia finally arrived in Sicily, ready for Cicero to take his new post, the two were as close as they could be, and eager to make the best of their new island home. But as Cicero fell deep into his work, learning the ins and outs of the island province's administration and Terentia struggled to settle down in a foreign land of mostly Greek speakers, the island began to feel less like an adventure and more like a prison.

"When do we return to Rome?" Terentia began to ask with a regularity that made it less of a question and more of an imperative. When Cicero finally rose to quaestor and became even busier at work, things grew worse between him and Terentia. Cicero knew Terentia was bored and lonely, but he was working for their future in a big job that would make or break his plan to step up to the next level of public office. Cicero did his best to balance work and life, but with progressively less time to commit to his homesick wife, he began to fear that she would leave him behind and return to Rome alone. But then Terentia became pregnant. In an instant, their worries faded and they came back together with a sense of mutual purpose.

Just before their daughter was born, Terentia's sister traveled to Syracuse to help care for the child. Having her sister around provided great joy for Terentia and quelled some of the pangs of homesickness. Cicero too was renewed in spirit by the birth of their daughter. Unfortunately, as well as his family life was going, his professional life was suffering. Of course, that was of Cicero's own doing.

Overlooking the white-capped sea stretched out before him, Cicero unfurled a blank scroll and dipped his quill in the ink-well. He looked on the blank page and thought, if only he could have this conversation in person, perhaps then he could be talked out of stirring up another hornet's nest. But such was not possible, so he began to write.

Gaius Julius Caesar—

My friend, I write in good spirits to inform you of an addition to my family in the form of a baby girl. We have named her Tullia Ciceronis. Terentia and baby are both doing well.

How is Rome? The heat of these summer months can drive a man insane. In Syracuse, the sea gives us much relief, so at least we have that over you uppity Romans. Truly though, how is the city? I know I ramble in regularity on the subject, but I do miss it. I am well liked here, perhaps more than in Rome, but I am not one of the people, so I fear it will never feel like home.

Why such time without a letter from you? I do hope dispatches have been reaching you. If not for your friendship alone, then for your counsel I eagerly await your reply. In the course of my duties I have uncovered details of a public official's poor handling of funds. I know you'd counsel to leave it be and not make another enemy, but absent you being here to actually state such, I know my nature will see me do the politically unwise and act. Of course, the odds are that I will do so regardless of your or anyone's advice, but I should like to hear your opinions regardless.

Do write soon, my friend.

—Marcus Tullius Cicero, Quaestor of the Province of Sicily

Cicero looked over the letter a moment, checking for mistakes and letting the breeze dry the ink. Satisfied, he rolled the scroll up, tying it closed with a strand of twine. He had his wax and stamp with him, but the wind moving through would never allow for a candle to melt the wax, so he opted to pack everything away and seal the scroll at home.

Tucking away the scroll, Cicero looked at the stack of bound papers he also took from his satchel and read: "In Verrem."

Walking home, Cicero passed through the town square again. It was getting late and he should have been home long ago, but he was enjoying the stroll enough that he'd actually done a full loop to keep it going. He just didn't want to have to think about the decision he had to make, so he looked out over the water at the setting sun and continued to take in the peaceful scenery.

"Sir Cicero," Cicero heard from behind as he turned to find his friend from the fruit stand. "You are well?" Septimius asked.

Cicero smiled. "I am, thank you."

Septimius approached, speaking in a quiet but direct tone. "Thank you for helping us," he said, looking over his shoulder, the volume of his voice lowering further. "Verres, he is bad man. He takes from all of us."

Cicero nodded. Verres, the provincial governor of Sicily was not well liked by the locals, whom he frequently shook down for excessive taxes. Cicero had heard inklings of such dealings when he first came to Sicily and had certainly noticed the sour mood of the local vendors, but it was not until Cicero became quaestor that he knew for sure.

As quaestor, Cicero managed the local administration, tracking and logging all taxes in and all payments out to the central government. As he looked into the scrolls, everything appeared on the up and up, but the more he became immersed in the local culture, the more he heard of Verres's "special" taxes from angry business leaders. Though Verres had certainly not been ordered to raise the taxes in the region, doing so was not such a serious offense. But as Cicero delved into the financial ledgers, the true problem became clear. If Verres was taking in extra taxes, they were not making their way into the general fund.

"You need more folks to talk to?" Septimius said to Cicero. "More. I can bring more."

"You have done enough already," Cicero said.

"So, you stop Verres?" the vendor said. "You make so he stop taking so much?"

Cicero had not intended to look into Verres's dealings. Investigating the provincial governor was not exactly the best way to make an ally of him, and living outside the political circles of Rome meant Cicero needed every ally he could get. Unfortunately for Cicero, reconciling his duties as quaestor with his political fortunes became progressively more difficult, as whispers of Verres's maleficence persisted.

It started with a murmur here and there, as Cicero overheard the Sicilians bellyache about the local government. Cicero was an outsider, so nobody came to him directly at first, but as time went on and he became known, some of the locals started to approach him. First and foremost of the informers was his fruit vendor, Septimius.

Septimius and Cicero had nothing in common but kindly manners and pleasant dispositions. It proved enough. Once Septimius knew he could trust Cicero, he inundated him with stories of Verres abusing his power for personal gain, as he threatened locals with the wrath of the Roman legions lest they not pay tribute to their tyrannical governor. Soon, Septimius was bringing all his friends to tell Cicero their stories of Verres and then those friends brought *their* friends and Cicero found himself where he stood now.

"I am looking into everything Verres has done," Cicero told Septimius.

"Is not enough to look. Verres must stop," Septimius said with a polite fervor.

It was clear that if Cicero wanted someone to talk him out of making another political enemy, Septimius was not the man for the job.

Chapter Thirteen

As night fell, Cicero approached his villa at the center of Syracuse. Perched high on a rocky crag, getting to and from his home was a bout of exercise, but the views that stretched well beyond the city and to the sea were certainly worth the exertion. Built of rock and earthen plaster, the walls of the villa were adorned in a bright white that matched the rest of the gleaming city. And though Syracuse was a bustling provincial city, all the clamor and chaos of such was left behind as Cicero opened the front gate and entered into the estate.

Stepping into the courtyard, Cicero was taken with the calm sanctuary of the gardens within. Lit with oil lamps, the many plants within projected crooked shadows across the open space. His mind burdened, Cicero still marveled at the beauty of his surroundings. It may not have been Rome, but the villa was certainly the nicest home he had ever lived in.

Pushing open the door to the house, Cicero heard a baby's cry within.

"Cicero, is that you?" Terentia called out from another room.

"It is," Cicero said, as Terentia stepped into the great room with their child in hand.

"Someone wants to say goodnight to you," Terentia said, as she handed over a groggy, squirming Tullia. At once Cicero was overtaken with guilt and joy. The guilt came on as he realized he had not even thought to make it home in time to see his baby daughter before she went to bed, but the joy of holding her quickly washed it away as Cicero kissed her on the forehead and she cooed up at him.

"That's all you get. To bed she goes." Terentia asked, lifting Tullia from Cicero's arms. "You're well?"

"I suppose," Cicero said.

Terentia looked at Cicero with concern, then called out down the hall. "Attia? Attia, can you put Tullia to bed for me?"

From down the hall, Terentia's sister Attia emerged and took Tullia off to bed swiftly. She knew the new parents had much to talk about.

As Attia disappeared down the hall without a word, Cicero kissed Terentia on the cheek. "I apologize for my tardy entry," he said.

"You needn't. We are fine. What of your work?" Terentia asked.

Cicero hedged.

"So, you've resolved to go through with it?" Terentia asked.

"I've resolved nothing, but I also don't see what choice I have," Cicero said.

"You always have a choice," said Terentia. "You have a family and a career. You should choose those."

"But those are exactly the reasons I have to go through with it all. How can I look at my family with eyes that have seen wrongdoing and yet my body did nothing to stop it? How can I expect the trust of the people when I do not work for the betterment of the republic?"

158

"And what happens when you have no eyes to look upon your daughter?" Terentia said.

Cicero started to respond but fell silent. A knock at the door gave him a reprieve.

"Just a moment, let me see who it is," Cicero said, walking to the door. "We have all night to discuss this." Cicero opened the door and his stomach dropped. It was Verres.

"Mr. Cicero. It seems we have much to discuss," Verres said.

Cicero led Verres to a table at the center of his study. The largest room of the house, a high ceiling sat atop walls covered in scrolls and scroll-laden shelves. This was Cicero's oasis, where he could go at any time to be alone with his thoughts and the thoughts of the greatest minds of his and many other generations. A shame to sully such a room with the presence of such business, he thought as they sat.

"It is a lovely villa," Verres said. "I lived here for a bit, you know."

"I did not," Cicero said.

"It was when I first moved to the province," Verres said. "I liked being able to look over all whom I control."

It took all Cicero's willpower to not openly scoff at Verres's condescending view of the people he was entrusted to govern. Did he not realize that he was their servant and not the other way around?

"Yes, it is a lovely home, in a lovely province, surrounded by many lovely people," Cicero said.

Tall and slender, Verres stared blankly back. A calm, fastidious man, Verres betrayed little of his emotions. "Tell me about this…project you've been working on," Verres said.

Cicero took a breath. "It brings me no joy, sir."

"So, you are investigating me," Verres said.

"I had no choice, sir," Cicero said, shifting in his seat.

"You seem nervous. You needn't be. I'm sure there is a perfectly reasonable explanation for any concern you might have. Just ask me your questions and we can be done with all this discomfort," Verres said, as he leaned back, staring calmly at Cicero. If he was concerned, his manner did not betray such.

Cicero considered a moment, searching for the most tactful way to broach the subject. "As quaestor, I am to manage the ledgers of our tax dollars."

"Yes, of course. I look at those same ledgers. They are clean and well kept," Verres said. Verres retained a calm demeanor, but Cicero could not ignore the swiftness of his retort. He may be projecting composure, but there was distress below the surface.

"I agree, sir," Cicero said.

"Then why the concern?" Verres said.

"Because all the income is not reported on the ledgers," Cicero said, seeing a twitch of Verres's eye.

"Of course it is," Verres said. "Everything is in accordance with the tax rates passed down to us from Rome."

"But those are not the only taxes you are taking in," Cicero said.

Verres's façade cracked, as he leaned in toward Cicero. "I have done nothing of the sort," Verres said with the slightest of scowls.

"I have reports too numerous to not delve into, sir," Cicero said.

"Reports?" Verres said with a laugh, his stony façade crumbling to reveal the anger within. "And I suppose those reports are coming from the provincials?" Verres calmed himself again. "Cicero, you cannot trust those people. They are not Romans."

"I was a provincial once," Cicero said.

"Ah, so there it is," Verres said with a sneer. "You're just a provincial trying to settle an old score. You've drummed it all up just to feel superior to your Roman betters. That's why you're doing all this."

"No, sir. I just hate a bully," Cicero said with a sternness that surprised him as much as it did Verres. "And it is my duty to the republic and all the people within it, be they in Rome or in one of her provinces."

"So, then you have already made up your mind?" Verres said.

"Not until you just helped me, sir," Cicero said.

Verres's face cracked a hateful smirk, as he stood and said, "Then I suppose there is no point in continuing our conversation."

Cicero went to stand as well, but Verres shoved him back into his seat.

"I suppose you'll be making your way to see the praetor tomorrow," Verres said glowering down on Cicero. "Perhaps we shall see each other on the way."

Leaning right into Cicero's face, Verres's naked anger dominated his once-calm exterior. "Please tell your wife and daughter good night for me. You have such a lovely family, Cicero. It must be a terrible burden knowing all you have to lose."

With a final shove, Verres turned to the door. Cicero watched him leave, terrified that he may have provoked a monster.

Cicero moved briskly through the empty streets of early morning Syracuse. Looking over his shoulder, he turned back and ducked down a side alley. It was not his normal route, but he suspected Septimius would forgive the absence of his usual visit given the circumstance.

Cicero had left his villa before first light, sneaking out from a side gate and ducking through an alleyway to get to a main street unseen. He had not seen any of Verres's men outside his villa, but it seemed prudent to be as cautious as possible, because at this point, getting his evidence to the praetor was the only choice he had.

Abstaining from sleep, Cicero had gathered his materials throughout the night and prepared to step out at first light. Despite not joining her in bed, Terentia never once came out to check on Cicero, which would be concerning under normal circumstances, but was more of a relief in this situation. Cicero had to take his evidence to the praetor whether Terentia wanted him to or not. Verres, unable to control his anger, had overplayed his hand and had given Cicero no choice in the matter.

Immediately after Verres's exit, Cicero sent his servants out to call up as many loyal guards as possible to keep his family safe, but such meant that Cicero would have to make his way this morning without accompaniment. Perhaps it was better to be alone, so as to go unseen in the streets, but as Cicero made his way he felt exceptionally vulnerable.

As the cobblestone road lurched upward, Cicero skipped along. He was close to the praetor's villa now and, having seen no sign of Verres's men, he was starting to feel more at ease. Perhaps Verres left last night confident that he had intimidated Cicero into submission. Whatever the case, as Cicero neared the crest of the hill, he did not let up on his pace. With his family threatened, he had to reach the praetor and get his support to gain the protection of the legionaries against revenge from Verres.

Cicero skidded to a stop at the pinnacle of the hill and his stomach dropped. Before him, just a stone's throw away, waited Verres and a gang of rough-hewn men. Making immediate eye contact with Verres, Cicero had no chance to retreat.

"Good morning, Cicero," Verres said, the situational upper hand allowing the return of his calm demeanor. "Thought I'd be seeing you this morning."

"Now, hang on, Verres," Cicero said. "If you hurt me, there will be questions."

"There will be far more questions if I do not," Verres said, stepping closer to Cicero.

"You can't just accost a quaestor and expect to get away with it," Cicero said, but he knew his words were hollow. He had given Verres little choice but to try to stop him by force.

"I'll take my chances," Verres said, reaching out to grab Cicero by the robe.

Verres halted, surprise drifting across his face, as something behind Cicero caught his attention.

Cicero turned to find Septimius approaching with a handful of men.

"Good morning, Sir Cicero," Septimius said.

"Leave here at once. I am a governor of Rome. I run this province and I have business with this man," Verres barked to Septimius and the other men.

"We will not leave," Septimius said.

"Then you will be dispelled by force," Verres said, nodding to his thugs to proceed.

Cicero turned to Septimius and his men. "Just go. You needn't be harmed too."

"We are here for Sir Cicero and we are here for ourselves," Septimius said, as more men poured in from an alley behind the thugs.

"All of you, leave now and you will not be punished," Verres said.

"We will not leave," Septimius said, as more men came in from another alley, then another.

Verres's thugs circled around him grew worried as the mob of Sicilian civilians surrounded them. The mob was nothing but food vendors and old men, but their numbers and stern resolve were enough to shake Verres and his men.

"Sir, maybe we should go," a thug said to Verres, as the mob closed in around their small group.

"No, we can't," Verres said, but his men were already throwing up their arms and easing out of the crowd until Verres stood alone.

Septimius looked to Cicero. "You wish to hit him first, Sir Cicero?"

Cicero couldn't help but smile at the exceptionally polite offer of violence, but he shook his head. "No, we should let him go. He will be dealt with as the law commands."

"Are you sure, Sir Cicero?" Septimius asked.

"I am," Cicero said.

Septimius shrugged, a little disappointed as he gestured to his men to open up a hole to allow Verres to leave. As Verres turned tail and fled, all the men he had stolen from bumped into him. As calm as he was in approaching Cicero, Verres was near tears as he finally escaped the mob.

Septimius looked to Cicero. "You want company on your walk, Sir Cicero?"

Cicero smiled. "Indeed I do."

Chapter Fourteen

In the weeks and months following Cicero's accusations against Verres, a trial was ordered and Cicero stood as prosecutor. Just as he did for each trial prior, Cicero wrote out his argument in painstaking detail. Unlike his prior trials, however, Cicero prepared with the confidence that came with his extensive training in the art of oratory. Finally, he felt like a true litigator.

The evidence Cicero had cultivated against Verres had breadth and depth, and he came into the proceedings with the support of a Roman Senate that had grown tired of the corruption Verres represented. Verres, however, was not going down without a fight.

With the considerable, if ill-gotten, means available to him, Verres sought out the best legal counsel, topping his brain trust with the finest orator in the republic: Quintus Hortensius Hortalus. If he was to stand trial, Verres was going to give himself every opportunity to come out on top.

Going into court Cicero fought the shaking hands and nerves that had hung over him all his life, but such was not indicative of a lack of confidence. After his successful defense of Sextus Roscius, Cicero had become something of a celebrity to the common folk. And after the Roman authorities saw the case he was to present against Verres, Cicero gained the respect of the elites as well. Finally, he was not seen as some gadfly upstart but as a serious man. Even so, nothing to do with the trial went as planned.

Prepared to argue his case on multiple levels and in various speeches, Cicero's plans were put on hold as Verres and Hortalus instituted a plan of indefinite deferral. Facing a pool of judges made not just of sitting senators but known reformers, Verres saw a smattering of unsympathetic faces that would surely not lean his way.

On the first day of the trial, Cicero used his considerable oratory skills to attack Verres, not directly on the crimes he was being charged with, but to paint him as a man with a history of corruption stretching the length of his life. It was a thorough takedown, but it would be the only argument Cicero would give against Verres.

After Cicero's damning opening salvo, Hortalus and Verres resorted to their delay tactics and argued for recess after recess, citing obscure, forgotten laws to help delay the inevitable. First, it was a law about conducting trials during important festivals, then Hortalus reached into obscure religious laws. The tactics were as absurd as they were effective, resulting in more than a year hiatus between the start and finish of the trial. With the delays, Hortalus hoped to test the attention span of the court and the public and eventually see the charges dropped in a haze of disinterest. Unfortunately for Hortalus and his client, Cicero was also a savvy legal tactician.

Working the political sphere, Cicero applied pressure to Verres and Hortalus, putting all aspects of their lives under intense scrutiny. With their respective business interests and personal wealth at stake, Hortalus informed Verres that they could delay no longer. They had to go to trial and risk losing or make a deal. Verres made a deal.

In the end Verres avoided an admission of guilt, taking a no-contest plea and agreeing to a permanent exile from Rome. Cicero had won but did so without the satisfaction of defeating Verres in court with all his carefully crafted arguments. Hollow though the victory felt, it was a victory over a powerful regional governor, and it vaulted Cicero into the lofty heights of public power.

As a provincial governor, Verres was not just a member of the Roman Senate but one with both voting and speaking rights in the chamber. By defeating such a man in court, Cicero was entitled by law to the legally vanquished man's standing in the Senate. Cicero may not have been able to use his well-honed oratory skills in court, but he could now use them in the biggest political arena in the Republic: the Senate.

One trial had brought Cicero to the attention of the people but sent him and Terentia into exile, and now another brought them back and made them of the elites. Unfortunately, the path to get there had damaged their relationship.

Cicero and Terentia strolled down the street in silence. Had she not heard him, he wondered to himself.

"That means Rome," Cicero said. "It means power and status. I will be in the upper reaches of the Senate. A true power broker."

Terentia continued walking but did not respond. Cicero started to speak, but a passing Sicilian man waved and called out to him. "Good day, Sir Cicero," he said with an admiring smile.

If Cicero had been well thought of by the Sicilians before he took Verres to trial, he was now revered.

"This is an opportunity to really make a mark and fight for the republic. It's what I've always wanted," Cicero said.

Terentia looked to Cicero with a sad smile. "Then I'm happy for you," she said, looking back to the path before her.

Cicero watched as she ambled along. Things had been strained, but he thought this news would bring her happiness and, he had hoped, get him back in her good graces.

"And you will have your family, your sister," he said. "You will be with them all again."

"Yes, that's true," Terentia said without looking to Cicero.

"I thought you'd be happy about it," he said.

Terentia looked to him coldly. "I'm surprised you thought about me at all."

Cicero absorbed the dig. Over the years he had successfully honed his abilities of expression and persuasion with the aim of swaying the minds of jaded politicians and powerbrokers, yet he could not evoke the slightest expression of joy from his own wife.

"I know I've been distracted, but you are never far from my thoughts. You and Tullia are the most important things to me," Cicero said.

Terentia kept walking without a word.

"Did you hear me?" Cicero asked.

Terentia stopped. "I did, I just didn't believe you."

"How can you say that?" Cicero asked.

"How can you say otherwise?" Terentia said. "I asked you not to continue with that case."

"He was stealing from the people and using his position in the republic to do so," Cicero said. "What choice could a good man have in that situation?"

"And what of the choice of a good husband?" Terentia asked, as she and Cicero stopped along the cobblestone street in front of their villa. Cicero studied her face, seeing marks of strain and lines of worry he had not noticed before. How long had she been looking at him like this, he thought to himself.

Cicero reached out to take Terentia's hand when the door to the villa swung open, revealing the square jaw and sturdy shoulders of a Roman legionary.

"Quaestor Cicero?" the legionary called out with a force that had been ingrained by years of training.

Cicero looked at the legionary, then past him to the line of other red-cloaked Roman soldiers lining the walkway of the villa behind him.

"I am, but why are you here at my home?" Cicero asked. Throughout the trial, legionaries had stood guard at the villa. Their presence was as comforting as it was necessary in the face of Verres's threats, but since the trial there had been no need for such measures.

"I am to bring you inside, sir," the legionary barked.

"I appreciate your services, soldier, but I can assure you that your protection is no longer needed," Cicero said.

"I do not protect you, sir. I protect Dictator Sulla," the legionary said tartly.

Cicero looked on with trepidation. What fresh mess had he stirred up now? Indeed, Verres had been a Sulla supporter, but more as a means of self-preservation than any true loyalty. But looking at the soldiers who had let themselves into his home and were now barking orders at him, Cicero was starting to question such an assessment. As the weight of the moment sunk in, Cicero remembered Terentia by his side and saw the lines of strain and worry on her face deepening.

"Go," she said. "Your work calls."

∼

Cicero walked through his home flanked by a pair of legionaries, their stomps echoing through the halls. The crisp impact of each step startled Cicero anew as he wondered how they were not cracking the marble beneath their feet. Turning toward the study, the men motioned Cicero in, but halted at the door, turning about face and standing as sentries.

As Cicero entered, he slowed to see a man with a shock of white hair and the thin, spindly shoulders of old age. Beneath the marks and furrows of age on the man's face, Cicero saw the remnants of a man he once knew.

"Hello, Cicero," Sulla said, bracing against his chair as he stood to greet the man visiting him in his own home.

"Hello, sir," Cicero said. "You look well."

"And it seems you still cannot lie convincingly," Sulla said with a smirk that did nothing to quell Cicero's embarrassment. "I appreciate the manners, but I see my old age in the reactions of everyone that sees me for the first time in years."

Cicero smiled. For all their differences, Cicero had always liked Sulla's frank, self-effacing manner. "Perhaps," Cicero said. "Or, perhaps they're just so happy to see you that they're thrown from their normal expressions."

Sulla smiled. For all their differences, he had always enjoyed Cicero's polite honesty and quick wit. "Yes, let us just assume that such is true so I can go on enjoying the rest of my day," Sulla said. "Please, sit, my friend," Sulla motioned to a guest chair, as he sat behind Cicero's desk.

Cicero obliged, appreciating that even with his advancing age, the great man still jockeyed for the position of power.

"I must admit that I am surprised to see you, sir," Cicero said.

"Well, I did not inform you of my visit, so *I* am not surprised," Sulla said. "Do you know why I am here?"

"I can only guess, sir," Cicero said. "But I suspect I have somehow reinserted myself as a thorn in your side. Perhaps I took upon my prosecution of Verres with more zeal that you appreciated."

"Verres?" Sulla said with a laugh of genuine surprise. "He is as empty as the robes he wears and not worth the fabric used to make them."

Cicero nodded, not sure what was going on.

"Does that surprise you, Cicero?" Sulla said. "Of course, I know of your prosecution, but knowing about it is the entirety of how it has affected me. I am the greatest man of the Roman republic. Perhaps you hold yourself with an esteem that does not match the effect you are capable of."

Cicero nodded, sufficiently put in his place. "I apologize, sir," he said.

"Nonsense," Sulla said, returning to his fatherly tone now that the hierarchy had been established. "We are just two men talking. No need for such postures," Sulla lied. "With all of this behind you now, I imagine you will be returning to Rome."

Cicero looked at Sulla, not sure how to respond. It was Sulla who had sent him away from Rome in the first place, so was Sulla here to remind him of that and make sure that Cicero would not return?

"Are you not yet decided on your plan, Cicero? I must say, such is not like you," Sulla said, expecting a prompt reply.

"I—I, I had considered returning to the city—"

"Perhaps I should tell you why I am here," Sulla said, pausing. The break in the conversation continued, causing anxiety to well up in Cicero as he wondered if he had missed a cue to say something. Finally, Sulla broke eye contact and spoke. "I am stepping down," Sulla said.

Without a beat, Cicero responded, "I am sorry to hear that, sir."

Sulla sat up, taken off guard. "I'm surprised to hear *you* say that."

"Why is that, sir?" Cicero asked.

"Because you are too bad a liar not to mean it," Sulla said.

"But what about the sentiment surprises you?" Cicero said.

Sulla studied Cicero. Cicero could see the cloudy beginnings of encroaching age starting to rob Sulla of his sight. Finally, Sulla spoke.

"Are you just being coy or are you not as smart as I remember?" Sulla said.

"I'm sorry, sir," Cicero said. "I understand that perhaps you think I do not like you and do not approve of you, but such could not be less true."

"And yet you have chosen to criticize me at every turn," Sulla said.

"Not you, sir. Just your methods," Cicero said.

Sulla mulled the words a moment. "Why do I feel like the victim of the coy mockings of a smarter man?" he asked.

Cicero took a moment to consider his response. Sulla was a man with great vanities, and Cicero would be wise not to offend him.

"I have never and will never mock you, sir," Cicero said. "You are a man of great weight and ability and my respect for you has never wavered, even when I disagreed with your actions."

Sulla nodded, satisfied. "Even when I took power in Rome?" he asked.

"Yes, sir," Cicero said. "Even then."

"And why is that?" Sulla asked.

"Because you were only doing what you thought needed to be done," Cicero said.

"That is true. The republic was broken when I took power, and all I have done since is reform it to stand on its own," Sulla said. "You agree with that?"

"Yes, sir," Cicero said.

"And would it surprise you," Sulla said, "that after taking power by force and pushing my agenda, I am going to step aside and return the republic back to senatorial control, just as it has always been?"

"I expected no less, sir," Cicero said.

Sulla again studied his counterpart. "So, Cicero," Sulla said. "I hope you will excuse me when I say that I am baffled. I am baffled not by your words, but your sentiment. I took power, but I did good with it. I forced changes, but they were all reforms that serve to reinforce the republic and allow for it to continue on in perpetuity. And yet, with all that good, you still believe I never should have done the little bit of bad necessary to make it all so?"

"Respectfully, sir, that is exactly what I believe," Cicero said.

Sulla sat back, forcing a laugh as he smacked the table with his hand. "Well, dear boy, you are certainly going to have to explain that one, because for the life of me I do not understand it."

Cicero considered a moment, gathering his thoughts. He looked at Sulla with plain sincerity. "I am not worried about you, sir. I am worried about the man who comes after you," Cicero said.

Sulla's forced grin faded, replaced by a worried expression.

"You are a good man, sir," Cicero said. "Honorable. That is not and should never be in dispute. I believe you wanted power, but I also believe you wanted to do good with it. In the end you used one to do the other, and there is great honor in the outcome of it all. But for all you've done to protect and solidify the republic, all you've done to reform its workings and improve its processes, your very path has undermined it all."

Sulla took a moment to digest Cicero's words. He took a breath. "Assuming that is true, how did my path undermine it?" he asked.

"I say this all with absolute respect, sir—"

"Set aside the pleasantries, Cicero," Sulla said. "You are walking out of here unscathed. If you are going to speak, speak earnestly. How did my path undermine the republic?"

Cicero took a breath. "You showed that the system can be defeated," Cicero said, letting his words hang in the air a moment.

"You showed that the laws can be cast aside and that a man can take power and institute his will," Cicero said. "With you, your will was the betterment of the republic. And maybe the next man to take power by force will do the same. Maybe he will use his military might to gain power, and maybe he will do nothing but good with his lofty status. But eventually one of them will not. The republic is about the will of our great society. The republic represents all of Rome, but now every person within it knows that one man can overwhelm the rest of us and claim it as his own. It is just a matter of time before one such man does so, and then there will be no going back."

Cicero stopped, as Sulla slumped in his seat. Minutes passed without a word. Finally, Sulla took a breath and looked at Cicero with a piercing gaze.

"Then," Sulla said, "we must hope you are wrong, Cicero."

"I do," Cicero said. "But I fear I am not."

"And what will you do if you are right?" Sulla asked.

Cicero considered a moment. "I'll fight it," he said.

"If all of the republic is impossible to stop, then why bother fighting?" Sulla asked.

"Because it is worth fighting for," Cicero said.

Chapter Fifteen

Cicero looked up from the pile of documents on the table before him at a group of plebes waiting in line with orderly patience to fill their water vessels at a public fountain. At the front of the line, a rickety, aging man looked on worriedly at the weak trickle of water coming from the spout. Normally, there would be no wait, as the entire line of people would be able to fill their vessels in the collecting pool below the spout. Of course, normally there would also be so much water pouring out into the pool that most of it would go over the sides and drain elsewhere or out into the Tiber. *Normally*.

Cicero went back to his papers and continued reading, stealing an occasional glance up at the water situation before him. As praetor, Cicero was tasked with many responsibilities in the judiciary sector, as well as some passed down from the consular level. As a stepping-stone and proving ground to consul, serving as praetor was as much an honor as it was a colossal undertaking. He would have to prove capable of moving up to the top level as well as master all the requisite knowledge so as to prepare for the burden of such a position. Even so, Cicero could not help but steal glances at the people waiting in line for the water that barely poured from the spigot.

Finally, Cicero set aside his papers and made his way to the group of plebes. As Cicero approached, he saw the older man at the spout snatch up his amphora and prepare to leave, either deciding that he had had enough or succumbing to the frustration of the minuscule trickle available to him. Cicero approached the man.

"Excuse me, but may I inquire as to the situation with the water?" Cicero asked.

"What is there to inquire about?" the man scoffed. "There is no water. It is plain to see—"

The man stopped himself at once, recognizing Cicero, or at least recognizing the advanced station Cicero's clothing represented.

"Excuse me, sir," the man said. "I meant not to bellyache."

"And one need not apologize for a bellyache," Cicero said. "And certainly not when it comes from such a frustration. The spout…has it always been so stingy with its offerings?"

The man looked Cicero over, not sure how candid he should be.

"Worry not," Cicero said. "I want only to help. Has there been an attempt by the government to fix the water spout?"

"Yes, of course. I am sure this is just temporary," the man said in a stilted, uncomfortable manner. Cicero saw that he was still not at ease.

"As I see you are a man of great honor and would never complain, I must ask, what have you heard others say?" Cicero said. "Just the words being spoken, not the names of anyone that might be speaking them."

The man nodded, understanding the bargain Cicero was striking with him.

"I have heard people swear against the Senate for not doing their job," the man said. "This spout worked well while Sulla was in charge. Nobody could complain about it, because we didn't know of a reason to. The sand builds up in the aqueducts and if it is not maintained, it flows down and blocks the spouts."

The man, getting worked up, soon forgot his reluctance to speak. "Sulla, he kept it working. But the Senate? They do nothing. They do nothing that does not bring them praise and glory. Build a bridge and they get to put their name on it. Clean the aqueduct and nobody knows the kindness you've done. Sulla gave orders and things were done. The Senate just fights amongst themselves and waits for someone else to do the work. And I—"

Catching his rising fervor, the man stopped. "But that is all I hear from others," the man said. "Never myself."

Cicero smiled. "Yes, of course not."

Light poured in from a skylight in the center of the Curia Cornelia roof, casting a beam of whiteness through the thin layer of smoke hanging in the Senate hall. At the edges of the room, oil lamps burned, filling in the dark corners of the space with flickering amber light. A lengthy, rectangular room, stepped levels up along the long walls dominated the space, leading to a slightly elevated landing at the fore. Men of varied but mostly advanced ages filled the space, their pristine white robes reflecting senatorial status. Cicero stood up to speak to the group.

"The people," Cicero said, holding a well-practiced Greek oratory posture, his arms angled to the side and tilted up. "Those whom we serve. Those who comprise this grand republic of ours. They are the power and we are their vessel."

Now a longstanding member of the Senate, Cicero spoke with a comfort and ease that his work as a lawyer had never allowed him to exhibit. He still got nervous before a big oration, but speaking weekly had made the process easier in ways his sporadic legal cases never could. He was simply more practiced now. Even so, there were new challenges from old foes that complicated the process.

"Just today," Cicero continued, "I was taken from my work to inquire of an assembly of citizens mired in wait for a faulty water spout—"

"Another *Cicero is the man of the people* lecture, is it?" a man called out from the other side of the room.

Cicero heard the jab but was used to them enough that he continued on without pause. "Gentlemen, who are we as senators of Rome if we are not taking care of the infrastructure that is our city?" Cicero said.

"You may be a senator, but you are no gentleman," another voice hollered, then echoed along the marble walls.

Cicero had spent his entire life absorbing jibes about his lack of noble and patrician blood, so these slights gave him no pause, but he knew they undermined his words. When he first joined the Senate, Cicero had only heard such comments as he walked past private conversations, but recently the attacks had become increasingly common, and there was no mystery why, Cicero thought, as he eyed not the people speaking the words but the man who provoked them: Catiline.

Following Cicero's successful defense of Sextus Roscius and the resulting attack on Catiline, Catiline left Rome in self-imposed exile. When the ill-will against him subsided, Catiline returned and put himself back in the political mix, gaining favor the only way he knew how: with money.

Working his way back into the Senate, Catiline built a coalition of supporters made up primarily of senators with dubious morals and of precarious financial standing whom he could help in return for their unquestioning support. When Cicero entered the Senate, Catiline's faction was already built and had never once voted for any of the issues that Cicero presented. Catiline himself had never so much as looked at Cicero, but his people certainly made life as difficult as possible for his former underling.

Nonetheless, Cicero was able to build a reputation within the Senate as a man of weight and substance, and as he took on the duties of praetor, his star burned as brightly as ever. But when Cicero and Catiline started working toward concurrent consulship bids, Catiline and his faction took every opportunity to make Cicero's life more difficult. The most glaring such example was their heckling during Cicero's orations, which were usually aimed at his lack of noble background.

"We are at a pivotal point," Cicero continued, "where we can build on the reforms Sulla put in place to solidify the republic, or we can let our political ambitions take the place of duties of office. It cannot be stated more plainly than that—"

"I think I speak for all when I say enough with the lectures of duty," Catiline said, rising.

"My time has not expired, sir. Nor have you been granted permission to speak," Cicero said.

"I may not have permission to speak, but I do not believe I am required to listen," Catiline said, motioning his minions to follow as he stepped away, leading half the room out with him. Cicero looked on as the stream of the departing drew all attention away from his speech.

The convening magistrate looked at Cicero. "Do you have more to say?" the magistrate asked.

Cicero looked on as the last of Catiline's men exited the room, his momentum leaving with them. He sighed and shook his head to the magistrate. "I do not," Cicero said.

As the senatorial chamber recessed and the remainder of the group made its way out, Caesar flagged down Cicero.

"Well, of what I heard, I liked what you had to say," Caesar said.

"Thanks, but it would have been nice to complete my thoughts," Cicero said.

"You're right though, the power of the republic sits with the people," Caesar said. "We need to curry favor with them if we wish to truly have power."

Cicero looked at Caesar askance. "I'm not sure you obtained my meaning," Cicero said. "I sought only to say that we owe it to them to take care of the business of Rome, not focus solely on the political moves that benefit our careers."

"Yes, of course," Caesar said. "That is also what I meant."

"But none of that will matter if I can't get an uninterrupted word in over Catiline," Cicero said.

"Well, you live to fight another day, regardless," Caesar said. "However, if you want to beat him out for consul, you'll need to figure out a way to get your words across without being interrupted."

Preoccupied with trying to find a solution for his continual Catiline problem, Cicero took the long way home to give himself longer to mull over the issue. After reaching his villa and doing ten laps around it, he finally gave up the task and headed home.

Entering the villa, Cicero found a servant feeding his year-old son, Marcus Minor, while Tullia, now ten years old, worked at her lessons across the table.

"Father," Tullia said, running to Cicero.

Cicero bent down to take her into his arms. "Hello, my dear," Cicero said. "How was your day?"

Tullia's smiled turned into a frown. "I'm having trouble with my studies," she said.

"Trouble?" Cicero said, "Dear me, what subject?"

"Oratory," she said.

"Well, then you are in luck, my love. I am a lover of the art. I would relish the opportunity to work on it with you," Cicero said, setting his daughter down. "You keep working and I'll come help after I talk with your mother."

"Miss Terentia is in the backroom, sir," the servant said.

"Very well, thank you," Cicero said, kissing Marcus minor on the forehead before making his way down the hall.

Entering the back room, Cicero felt Terentia's icy mood without her needing to say a word, which was fortuitous, because as she saw Cicero step in, Terentia said nothing to him.

Setting down his satchel, Cicero watched his wife put the finishing touches on what could only be a dress for a formal evening gala.

"You look lovely," Cicero said to no response. "To what event is this owed?"

"Flavia is hosting a dinner party," Terentia said without meeting her husband's eye.

"I do not recall hearing of this event," Cicero said.

Terentia finally looked to him, stone-faced. "Perhaps that is because you were not told of it," Terentia said, as she grabbed the last of her things and stepped out.

Cicero waited a moment, then followed her out. By the time he reached the great room, all that remained of Terentia's presence was the front door closing behind her.

Cicero sighed.

"Is it time to help with my studies now, Father?" Tullia asked.

Chapter Sixteen

Cicero looked on from his usual seat in the Senate hall, as Catiline bloviated about his business acumen as a self-made man, positing it as his primary qualification for the consulship. If Cicero were a lesser man, he would interrupt Catiline just as he had been interrupted yesterday. Cicero certainly had more impetus to do so, since Catiline's boasts of being a great businessman teetered on the line between gross exaggeration and an outright falsehood. The primary evidence of such was the glaring fact that Catiline had been born into a family of immense, multigenerational wealth. But more pertinent in Cicero's mind was that just a fraction of the fortune willed to Catiline remained, which was an odd state of affairs for a man with supposedly valuable businesses.

As Catiline prattled on, Cicero looked around the room at the many senators listening raptly. Catiline already had half the room in his pocket, and now it seemed the majority of the other half was taken in by his empty words. However, as well as Catiline had set himself up, he was not without his detractors.

As Cicero figured it, Catiline had been sued more than everyone in the Senate combined, with a few members of the

Senate having sued him personally. But one need not be involved in litigation with the short-tempered Catiline to dislike him, and Cicero took solace in knowing that the men who mattered did not like or support Catiline. Sadly though, Cicero thought to himself, there were precious few such men of substance left in the Senate chambers.

Walking home that night, Cicero veered from his normal path to walk by the waterspout that had drawn his attention the other day. Tonight, however, there was no line because there was no water. Cicero paused to look at the arid concrete making up the pooling space below the spout. What little water had flowed before had now ceased completely, and if the complete lack of moisture in the collecting pool was any indication, there had been no water for at least a full day.

Coming home, Cicero just wanted to retire to his study and read. Dinner could happen or not, but he would rather focus on something other than his thoughts. Instead, Cicero entered to find Tullia crying and the servant trying to calm her with one hand while she held Marcus Minor in her other arm.

"What's wrong, dear?" Cicero asked Tullia, as she kept crying.

"Bad day at school," the wet nurse said.

"Those happen," Cicero said. "Where's Terentia?"

The wet nurse hesitated, not sure what to say.

"Am I to understand she's gone then?" Cicero asked.

The wet nurse nodded.

"Very well," Cicero said. He kissed Marcus Minor on the head and looked back to the wet nurse. "Can you tend to him while I talk with Tullia?" Cicero asked, motioning to his crying daughter.

The wet nurse nodded and disappeared down the hall.

Cicero bent down to Tullia. "Trouble at school, my dear?" Cicero asked.

Tullia nodded but said nothing.

"Oh dear," Cicero said. "Did someone take your voice from you?"

Tullia smiled and wiped away a tear. "I have my voice," she said.

"Thank the gods," Cicero said. "Well, if you have your voice, then I am certain nothing that transpired at school could possibly be worth fretting about so. What happened, my dear?"

"They made fun of me," Tullia said.

"Oh, my dear, I'm sorry. Sometimes kids say things that they don't mean," Cicero said.

"They meant it, Father," Tullia said. "They said we are not real Romans. They said I wasn't born here, so we're not real Romans."

Cicero looked at his daughter, remembering not so long ago when he had gone to his mother with similar concerns. "Come, my dear," Cicero said. "Let's go for a walk together."

Walking through the streets and alleyways, Cicero and Tullia meandered through the city. Far more intrepid than Cicero had been at her age, the precocious ten-year-old led the way, knowing the streets better than him. Whereas Cicero had been forced into independence, with Tullia, it was a natural trait. Cicero admired that about his daughter; he admired much about her.

Cicero hadn't much pondered fatherhood in his early life. Of course, he understood the benefits of being a father, but it was not until Tullia came into his life that he really understood the spiritual gifts of children. Even so, it was not something he'd ever had much luck articulating in conversation or in writing.

"To the right, my dear," Cicero said, directing Tullia to a street winding up one of the seven hills of Rome.

"Are we almost there?" Tullia asked, not complaining but driven by a curiosity to discover what lay at the end of their journey.

"Almost," Cicero said. "How long have the other children been giving you trouble, dear?"

"Not long," Tullia said, trudging along but trying to appear at ease during the strenuous climb. Since early in her life Tullia's stoic nature had been evident. The normal bumps and bruises that come with learning to use one's body usually evoked tears in children, as they also dealt with pain and fear, but not in Tullia's case. She had her moments, of course, but they were few and far between; when Tullia would encounter discomfort, she'd just swallow it and keep going. The older she got, such stoicism became less a surprise and more a defining characteristic. It took a lot to upset Tullia, which Cicero admired. But when she was upset, Cicero paid immediate attention because he knew it was real. Of course, that didn't make getting the information out of her any easier.

"Not long, huh? Does that mean weeks or months?" Cicero asked.

Winded from the climb, Tullia took in a deep breath and said, "Not long."

"You know, when I was your age, the kids were mean to me too," Cicero said.

Tullia slowed. Stealing a glance at her father she asked, "Really?"

"Oh, yes. I was very sick as a kid, so I was much smaller than the other kids when I was finally able to go to school," Cicero said.

"And they made fun of you for that?" Tullia said.

"They did. They'd push me around too. And that got worse when I started moving up to study with the older boys," Cicero said, motioning to a dirt path diverging from the street. "Up that way, dear."

Tullia obliged, taking in a breath but not slowing, even as the grade steepened. "Why did you study with the older boys?" she asked.

"Well, I may not have liked school because of all the bullies, but I loved learning. And I got so good at it that they had to put me in to study with the much older kids," Cicero said, growing winded himself. He peered up the sparsely wooded hill. Not too much farther.

"Can I do that too?" Tullia asked.

"If you want, my dear," Cicero said.

"Did they stop making fun of you when you got bigger?" Tullia asked.

"Well, they stopped making fun of me for that, but they never stopped giving me grief about not being born in Rome," Cicero said.

"Like me," Tullia said with an excitement that quickly faded. "Oh, but that means they'll keep making fun of me."

"No, no, that's not what I'm saying—"

Tullia started to cry. "They'll never like me, will they, Father?"

Cicero bent down, comforting his daughter. "Honey, it's fine," he said. "Some people will never be nice, and you're probably better off not to be liked by them because they're usually not good people."

"I want to leave," Tullia said, Cicero's argument not swaying her. "Can we leave? I want to leave Rome."

"Hold on, dear," Cicero said. "Just wait a moment. Let's sit down and talk about this."

"Sit down? But we need to keep going until we get to the secret place you're taking me to," Tullia said, her curiosity getting the better of her tears.

"My dear, we are already there," Cicero said, motioning Tullia to turn around and look on the whole of Rome stretching out beyond the hill. "Sit, my dear. Let's talk."

Leading Tullia off the trail to the grassy hillside, Cicero went to take a seat, paused, immediately reminded of sitting in just that spot all those years ago with his mother. He'd come to sit at this place many times since, but it was still that day with his mother that he remembered most vividly. As Tullia sat beside him, Cicero felt a pang of nostalgia as he missed his mother as if she just died all over again.

"What's the matter, Father?" Tullia asked.

"I just remembered sitting up here with your grandmother and it felt like it was not so long ago," Cicero said looking out at the city gleaming in the late day sun. "It makes me miss her all over again."

Tullia thought about Cicero's words a moment, then looked out on the city too. For a while, they sat in silence looking out on the hills and the roads and the buildings that somehow all came together to serve as home to more than a million people.

"What do you see, dear?" Cicero asked Tullia.

Tullia looked out on the city, then turned back to her father, not sure what he wanted to hear.

"Go on, tell me what you see," Cicero said.

"I see Rome," Tullia responded.

"What else?" Cicero pressed.

Tullia looked back out at the city with determination. She was going to figure out the right answer. "I see buildings," she said.

"What kinds?"

"All kinds."

"What do you see most of?"

"Homes."

"Who lives in those homes?"

"People."

"What kind of people?"

"Romans."

"Just like you."

Tullia furrowed her brow, confused. "I'm not a Roman," she said.

"Of course you are. I'm a Roman and your mother is a Roman, and so you are a Roman too," Cicero said.

"But I wasn't born here," Tullia said.

"You're right," Cicero said, as Tullia slumped. "But look at the city again."

Tullia obliged.

"Where does Rome start?" Cicero asked.

Tullia looked to the city, then to her father, then back to the city. It dominated the horizon. "I can't tell," she said.

"Me neither. Can you tell where it ends?" Cicero asked.

Tullia gave a cursory look, turning back to her father, shaking her head.

"I can't either," he said. "Look out once more. Do you see walls?"

Tullia peered out again and shook her head. "No," she said.

"That's right," Cicero said. "Because there are no walls around Rome, and that is because Rome is not just a city, it is the whole of its people." Cicero gestured toward the great city. "My dear, Rome goes on in every direction in distances you cannot fathom. Within it are rivers and mountains and seas and countless people that speak languages most people will never hear. It seems to me that a Roman who has only seen this city has not seen Rome at all."

Tullia took in the words but soon tucked them away to digest later, as the immediate task came to mind.

"Yes, but how do I get the kids to be nicer to me?" Tullia said.

Cicero laughed, enjoying his daughter's intense focus but also remembering the ruse he had used to draw the bigger boys into the alley with the tough plebeian kids. "Well, dear," he said, "I think that is up to you to figure out. But perhaps we should get you back home."

Cicero started to stand, but Tullia put a hand on his to stop him. "Can we stay for a little while, Papa?" she asked.

Cicero smiled and returned to his seat. "Of course we can," he said as Tullia cuddled up next to him and they looked out on the great city.

The next day Cicero woke early, hoping to give Tullia a pep talk and get her off to school. However, when he went to her room, Cicero found that not only was Tullia already awake, but she had fed herself and was working on her speech for class.

"Well, my dear, it seems I am no longer needed here," Cicero said.

Tullia finished writing out her thought then looked up at Cicero. "What did you say, Papa?"

Cicero smiled. "Just…good luck at school today," he said.

"Thanks. Is Mommy coming home today?" Tullia asked.

Cicero had hoped Terentia's absence would go unnoticed by Tullia. Increasingly, Terentia had been coming home late into the night, but to not come home at all was concerning, and it had kept Cicero up until the early morning. Maybe they had married too young, or were ill-suited to begin with, or Cicero's career was getting in the way, but clearly this was a situation that was only getting worse. Nonetheless, Cicero did his best to keep his concerns from Tullia.

"Yes, my dear, I'm certain she'll be home later," Cicero lied.

His mind focused on the absence of his wife, Cicero made his walk to work a little more distractedly than normal. Cicero asked Terentia's handmaiden about his wife's whereabouts but was told just that she was fine and was given no specifics about her location. Knowing Terentia was safe was a relief, but it was cold comfort overall. This kind of behavior could not be allowed. It was not fair to Cicero and it was not fair to their children. Cicero would make such known to Terentia when he returned home at the end of the day. But Cicero couldn't dwell any longer on his domestic problems at home; he needed to figure out what to do about his Catiline problem.

For all the advice Cicero had given to his daughter last night, he had little to give himself. Moreover, after seeing Tullia attacking her problem with such single-minded zeal, he was starting to think that maybe he should have been the one soliciting advice.

Despite his mind wandering toward his domestic concerns, Cicero retained the wherewithal to navigate the streets, making certain to pass by the faltering waterspout. Approaching the spout, Cicero found the area again empty, as citizens had obviously given up on it. As he passed through, Cicero saw the same cantankerous old man he had spoken with before lugging two water-laden buckets, spilling the sloshing contents as he walked heavily on the uneven cobblestone street.

"You've found new a new waterspout, I see," Cicero said to the older man.

"Hmm?" the old man said, perking up to see Cicero but souring as the strain of holding the buckets made him remember his situation. "Oh, no spout. Now we must carry it back from the Tiber."

Cicero looked to the green, murky contents of the bucket. There were many reasons aqueducts were built to bring water into the city, but paramount among them was that nobody could or should drink the water from the Tiber. Rome was many wonderful things, but none of its attributes helped keep the river clean. There were just too many people in Rome creating too much waste for the Tiber to be anything but a repugnant stream of filth.

"You can't drink that water, sir," Cicero said. "You'll be sick as certain as the sun will set tonight."

"With respect, Senator, maybe you can get by without drinking this water, but I haven't much choice," the cantankerous man said. "None of us do unless we want to walk half the city to find a working fountain."

Cicero started to respond, but stopped. The man was right and there was nothing Cicero could possibly tell him that he didn't already know. Finally, Cicero just shrugged.

"You're right. We've failed you," Cicero said.

The older man looked anxious. He wasn't used to hearing a politician talk this way, so he didn't know how to respond. Eventually his anger overpowered his good sense in the same way that had led to the scar at the bridge of his nose.

"Well, you're damn right I'm right. But I don't like hearing you say it," the older man said. "No disrespect to you, sir, since I can tell you're one of the good ones, but you senators are supposed to fix this stuff."

"You're correct, sir," Cicero said. "There is no excuse for our inaction on this and many other things."

"Hell, son, if you don't have an excuse, then there's no way it is getting fixed, is there?" the older man said.

"I wish I could do it myself, but it takes a vote of the entire Senate to get things like this done, and I can't get them all to listen to me," Cicero said.

"Well, they better start listening to you, or they're going to have to start listening to a whole lot of us," the older man said.

Cicero perked up. "There are a lot of you that are angry about a lot of things, aren't there?" Cicero asked.

"Yes, sir," the older man said. "There are a lot of us angry about just this one fountain, but if you open this discussion up to other things, you're looking at a city full of angry people."

Cicero considered this.

Hordes of merchants tended to customers along a busy market alleyway on the path to the Senate chambers, which were tucked between rows of tall apartment buildings. The sunlight on both ends of the market highlighted just how dark the shaded area in between was. With the many corner kitchens of the city opening soon, cooks filled the space, looking to purchase the raw goods necessary to feed Rome.

Getting to the front of the line, a young cook looked over the butcher's table, pointing to the cuts he was interested in. He tumbled forward into the butcher's stand along with everyone else in line as a train of senators sauntered through, their stout bodyguards shoving their way through to clear a path. At the head of the group was Catiline.

"The votes for us matter, but it's just as important that we take votes away from him," Catiline told his cohorts. "I don't just want Cicero to lose and I don't just want to embarrass him, I want Cicero's career ruined. I want him to lose so badly that nobody will ever stand in support for him again, lest they sacrifice their own political hopes."

Lentulus Sura, a sly, gaunt senator walked in lockstep with Catiline at the fore of the group.

"We're already in the process of making that happen," Lentulus said, "but there are other outcomes to consider. We need to be prepared if Cicero wins."

"He won't," Catiline said. "He can't. He does not have the support of the Senate, nor does he have the money to garner their support."

"Perhaps not," Lentulus said. "But the man is cunning."

Catiline nodded, considering Lentulus's notion, then shrugged it off.

"Cunning is fine, but I'll gladly take rich over it," Catiline said, as a clatter in the near distance roused their senses. They moved closer to the public square outside the Senate chambers, and the clatter turned to the discernible clapping of a large group.

"Is there a rally planned for today?" Catiline asked, as they rounded the corner and halted, a dense crowd of plebes impeding their progress. Catiline squinted beyond the crowd to a figure at the height of the Senate steps addressing the crowd: Cicero.

"…And I know your frustrations, because I have the same ones," Cicero called out to the crowd. "I see it every day, both on the streets of our city and in the halls of our government. Our roads and aqueducts beg for basic maintenance, but nothing happens because there is no political glory in fixing that which is already built. So, the profound inactivity of those you voted into office does not just continue, it grows stronger, as it prevents them from doing their most basic tasks. Help me change that."

The crowd cheered.

"Rome did not sprout from the soil a great society," Cicero continued. "It was built, brick by brick and road by road, by the hard work of Romans simply doing their duty to the republic. But it isn't just incumbent upon each and every one of us as Romans to maintain that standard, but also for those of us representing you in the Senate. It is the very requirement of our office."

The crowd cheered again, louder this time.

Catiline glowered at Cicero and the crowd a moment, then turned to Lentulus.

"Perhaps you're right," Catiline said. "It would be irresponsible not to consider all outcomes. Tell your men in Gaul we must speak." Catiline turned, leading his delegation from the square.

At the top of the Curia Cornelia steps, Caesar watched with the other senators as Cicero called out to the crowd and the crowd called back to him. While some in the group of legislators grumbled about the pressure that came with such a display, Caesar was impressed and intrigued with his friend's tactic. Brokering behind the scenes for power within the Senate chambers was important, but it was clearly not the only way to garner power in Rome.

"We work for *you*, my friends," Cicero said. "Do not forget that. We are your representatives, so tell us what you want until we give it to you or you should find new senators who will."

The crowd cheered as Cicero waved to them and stepped away. As he turned, Cicero saw that a congregation of his colleagues was looking at him. From within the group, Caesar approached.

"Well, I guess you found a way to have your voice heard," Caesar said.

Cicero shrugged.

"Not sure it will matter if nobody in the Senate will also listen," Cicero said.

"Nonsense," Caesar said. "You have cultivated something far more important than the support of the Senate. You have the ire of the people."

After the Senate session, Cicero made his way home. At least he tried to. Although his antics had ruffled feathers in the chambers, they had also made people aware of the effect of their collective inaction. Of course it helped that Catiline was absent from the proceedings, which allowed Cicero to address the Senate about the same concerns he had presented to the crowd. Accepting words of support from his colleagues, Cicero tried to make his way to the door, but each step found a new person wishing to talk with him. Eventually, Cicero cut short these conversations and navigated to the exit. His political career was important, but Cicero had family concerns to deal with.

Finally home, Cicero stepped in quietly, not wanting to disturb Tullia and Marcus Minor, who was playing in the great room under the supervision of his wet nurse. From the corner, Cicero watched as Tullia tried to play with her younger brother, but he mostly flopped around and put toys in his mouth. Regardless, Tullia managed to situate her dolls and figurines into an audience before her. As she prepared to read her speech from class to them, she spied her father watching from the other room.

"Father!" Tullia said, as Cicero came to hug her and her brother.

"I'm sorry to interrupt, my dear," Cicero said. "I see you're preparing to give a speech. Were you able to give it to your class today also?"

"I was. They liked it," Tullia said.

"So, they didn't give you a hard time?" Cicero asked.

"Those same boys tried, but I convinced them to stop," she said.

"And how did you do that?" Cicero asked.

"I reminded them that Rome has no walls," Tullia said matter-of-factly.

Cicero looked on her, trying to understand her answer. "Why would that make them stop being mean to you?" Cicero asked.

"Because I told them that we used to live with a barbarian tribe before we moved to Rome and that there was nothing to stop my barbarian friends from coming to the city and finding the people who are mean to me," Tullia said with a grin.

"But, my dear, that isn't true," Cicero said, not quite sure how to handle this.

"Yes, I know that, but they don't," Tullia said proudly. "Do you want to hear my speech?"

"I'd love to, my dear. And perhaps we can have a conversation about ethics after that," Cicero said, then he looked at the wet nurse. "Is my wife in yet?" When the wet nurse stared back silently, Cicero saw the concern in her eyes that he had been too busy to notice before.

"It's fine. I'm not mad at you, just worried about Terentia. When was the last time you saw her?" Cicero said.

"I saw her today, sir," the wet nurse said.

Cicero sighed.

"But she is already out for the night?" Cicero said. The wet nurse hedged, not certain how to respond, as she peered down the hallway. Cicero followed her gaze and marched down the hall and into their bedroom.

Entering the room, Cicero found nothing out of sorts. But then he noticed Terentia's wardrobe door ajar. Cicero opened it completely to find that it was completely empty. He opened the other wardrobe, which was also empty. Going around the rest of the room he found that everything of Terentia's was gone. Cicero sat on their bed and took a breath. He looked around at the vacant room, letting it all soak in.

"Father, are you ready for the speech?" Tullia called from outside the room. After a moment, Cicero steeled himself and walked out to his daughter.

Chapter Seventeen

Through clogged, congested streets, the procession moved at a steady pace, constricting and expanding as necessary on its snaking journey through the city. A handful of stout men led the way. Sometimes the men had to push their way through the crowd to clear a space and sometimes the crowd recognized the determination of the men leading the procession and wisely stepped back without being told. Although these men were former soldiers, none were in uniform, in accordance with the law barring such. Being in uniform would probably have made their peace-keeping efforts markedly easier, but law or not, that would simply not have gone over well with the public, especially because this parade was intended to introduce Rome's newest consul to the people.

As the parade marched into a large public square, they approached the Curia Cornelia building, which held the Senate chambers where the new consul, Marcus Tullius Cicero, would be inaugurated into office.

In the middle of the slow-moving caterpillar of people, Cicero took in the moment as best he could, but it was a bit overwhelming for a man more used to scrolls and quiet reflection than he was crowds and being the center of attention. Nonetheless, Cicero enjoyed the adulation and support of the crowd as he made the march to his consular inauguration and the completion of a dream he'd carried with him since childhood.

Since the early days after the monarchy fell and the republic was formed, incoming consuls walked this same path. Following such traditions, earlier this day Cicero had presided over the ritual sacrifice of some unfortunate animals. The sacrifice had not been his favorite event of the day, but tradition was tradition and Cicero was not going to stand in the way. After the sacrifice, the parade of senators and prominent citizens started their walk through Rome and to the Curia for the actual inauguration.

The tradition of the march through the city originated nearly five hundred years ago, and its intent was to introduce the incoming consul to the people he would be serving. While such was a nice way for the people to see their new leader and for the leader to see the people, Cicero's situation was something different. As a man not of noble or patrician blood, Cicero was an anomaly in the history of Roman consuls. Rarer still, Cicero had spent much of the recent months speaking directly to the people about their concerns regarding the republic, so he was not as unknown as the others had been.

As the parade moved into the Curia Cornelia square, the soldiers at the front moved to the side and Cicero led the procession toward the building. When Cicero approached, he saw Tullia and Marcus Minor to the side in the care of Terentia's sister, Fabia. Tullia waved emphatically to her father.

"Father! Father! You finished your parade!" Tullia said, nudging Marcus Minor to wave too. The toddler had the wherewithal to mimic his sister, but waved to *her* instead of their father.

Cicero smiled and looked at Fabia.

"Is Terentia not around?" Cicero asked.

Terentia's sister shrugged, not certain what to say. With the congregation moving inside, Cicero cut short the awkward exchange.

"Well, I thank you for making certain the children were able to attend," he said.

Cicero looked at his children. "But only the men of Rome may enter the Curia," he said kissing them on the foreheads. "You two must head home and get into bed now."

Cicero again kissed his children, then turned to continue his journey toward the senate chambers. Making his way toward the steps, Cicero slowed as two Gallic men at the edge of the crowd caught his attention. Completely motionless, the Gauls stood out against the lively crowd. As Cicero moved closer, the two men stepped out into the path.

"Ah, there you are," Caesar said, stepping before Cicero. "I've spent half the day trying to make my way up to see you."

"Caesar, you're here," Cicero said, looking beyond Caesar, searching in vain for the two menacing Gauls.

"Of course I'm here. I couldn't very well miss your inauguration," Caesar said, patting his friend on the shoulder.

"I thought perhaps you'd be hosting more games for the public or passing out grain in the Aventine," Cicero said, offering a friendly jab to his friend.

"The power is with the people, right?" Caesar said with a smirk. "I'm only following your lead, my friend."

Cicero nodded, hiding his concern. Cicero dealt with the public by trying to engage them in a discourse and understand their wants and needs. What Caesar was doing was buying their love. Even worse, Caesar was going into great debt to garner this love. Each of the games he hosted and every temple he repaired was done on credit. What happened when he had to face his creditors? It was dangerous for a man with the love of the people to be backed into a corner like that. But Caesar was a friend, so Cicero chose to give him the benefit of the doubt. Besides, this was a day to celebrate.

"Come now, let's get you inside. I cannot wait to see Catiline's face as you take your seat before the Senate," Caesar said, throwing an arm over Cicero and guiding him to the steps. As they walked, Cicero looked back to where the two Gauls were, but they were nowhere to be seen.

Catiline stood at the front row of the Senate chambers with Lentulus Sura and the rest of his cabal of sycophantic senators. Catiline struggled to keep stone-faced, but his bitterness bled out through his eyes, all but contorting his face into a stern frown as Cicero stood to take his oath. Across the chamber, Caesar smiled as he looked at Catiline's scowl. Meeting eyes with Caesar, Catiline immediately wiped off the scowl and straightened up, which only bolstered Caesar's enjoyment of the moment.

Before the entirety of the Senate and all the noble interlopers and power brokers, Cicero stood at the raised landing in the center of the room before the consul's seat.

"By guiltless blood I stand before you with all the Gods as my witnesses as I offer myself as the one who will prosecute the laws of Rome by the force of the republic. By sword, by fire, by any means hence, I shall protect this republic and all those who make it up or I shall perish in the effort," Cicero said to his august colleagues.

The chamber cheered and the senators came down from their seats to offer congratulations to the new consul. Too busy to see anything but the seemingly unending train of well-wishers thrusting themselves before him, Cicero did not notice Catiline and his companions make their way to the front of the line.

As Catiline and Lentulus moved closer to Cicero, Caesar stood still, noticing Catiline's hands hidden under the sleeves of his robe. Caesar cut through the crowd, trying to get to Cicero first. Just as Caesar was about to step in between Catiline and Cicero, a rotund senator wandered into Caesar's path. Caesar shoved him aside, certain he would find Cicero under attack as he came into view again. Instead, Caesar found Cicero and Catiline shaking hands, at which he breathed a sigh of relief.

"Congratulations, Consul. It was a hard-fought victory, but you deserve it," Catiline told Cicero, who was just as shocked to hear it as the approaching Caesar was. "I hope we can put the election behind us and work together," Catiline continued, as heads turned to see the interaction. "In the end, we're all just humble servants of the republic."

"Indeed, I could not share your sentiments more," Cicero said.

As Catiline smiled and headed off to the exit with his minions in tow, Cicero turned to Caesar.

"I didn't know it was possible to get such graciousness from such a graceless man," Cicero said.

"I think I'd rather the man spat venom. At least that would be honest," Caesar said.

"He has his supporters but not in the numbers that can get anything done. Not any more. He can join the coalition or fade into obscurity," Cicero said. "Honest or not, what choice does he have but to support me?"

"A man always has choices," Caesar said, but Cicero had already turned his attention to the line of men waiting to congratulate him. Caesar, however, did not take his eyes off Catiline, watching him as he headed outside, stopping to talk with two square-jawed Gallic men on the steps to the Curia.

Cicero had worked his entire life to get to the rank of consul, but now that he had officially taken office and was attending a feast in his own honor with all the great men of Rome, all he wanted was to go home and sleep. Preparations for the day had kept him from getting a good night's sleep for most of the week. That, coupled with a day walking through Rome engaging with everyone he encountered, had left Cicero exhausted as never before. It was an exhaustion that went far beyond taxing just his physical capacity; he was mentally exhausted too. Cicero had been unable to complete a physical task before, but straining to stay intellectually engaged was a new experience. But the custom was for the newly seated consul to sit and feast in celebration of his position, and Cicero was not going to disrespect the office just to get a little sleep.

So Cicero nodded as patrician landowners talked of the travails of exporting goods to Greece, doing his utmost to stay engaged.

"...and by the time it gets there, they tell me the oil is bad," the landowner babbled on. "How, I say? It's the dead of winter. It's so cold, it should be as fresh as the day it was pressed."

"Yes, well, perhaps we can have some independent verification on the other side. Maybe an office of the trading affairs in Athens is due," Cicero said, amazed that he was still making sense.

"Excuse me, my friend," Caesar said to the landowner, as he broke up the conversation. "I have some important Republic business to discuss with the consul." Caesar motioned Cicero to the side and they stepped away.

"Hope you don't mind," Caesar said, "but you looked ready to nod off mid-sentence."

"Ready? I do believe I fell into a slumber long ago," Cicero said, looking at Caesar blankly.

"Perhaps you should head home now. I would be happy to escort you," Caesar said.

Cicero offered him a confused smirk in return. "Citizen Caesar, am I to take this as an offer to court me? I should say, it is an offer of the like I have not ever received," Cicero said, as Caesar rolled his eyes.

"I don't trust Catiline to be the honorable man he seemed to be today. He made a real show of it to anyone around and I don't like that. Nor do I like him, but that's just the natural response to having met the man," Caesar said.

"I'll be fine. He is a bully and bullies are all bark and no bite. He doesn't have enough courage to try to hurt a consul of Rome," Cicero said.

"No, but he has enough courage to hire someone to do it for him," Caesar said. "Let me leave my man Magnus with you."

Caesar motioned to a grim-faced man standing with his back to the wall in the rear of the room, as sturdy as he was stern.

"Thank you, but no. I have my consular guards. They will more than suffice," Cicero said, taking a breath and trying to wake up a bit. "But I should get back to the party. I wanted this job, so now I have to deal with the realities of being the man who everyone wants something from."

≈

207

He stumbled along the cobblestone way, and anyone watching Cicero on his walk home would have been justified in assuming him more than a couple sheets to the wind. But despite reaching the pinnacle of his life's aspirations, which was more than enough reason to imbibe, Cicero had had just a few sips from his wine chalice, only doing as manners dictate when one is being toasted. Instead, Cicero was intoxicated only by a weeks-long sleep deficit.

Struggling to keeps his eyes open, Cicero followed the torches of his guards. The temptation to close his eyes grew greater with each step. Each time sleep threatened to engulf him, Cicero would startle awake, bug-eyed, only to quickly sink back into sleep.

Cicero blinked, then awakened to the bright torches of his guards. But as Cicero blinked once more, his eyes reopened to find the torches gone and himself at a T-junction in the road. Looking up at the rock wall blocking his forward progress, Cicero directed his still-dazed eyes left, then right as the guards jogged off in opposite directions. Cicero looked on, confused as the light from the torches faded away with the fleeing guards. His stomach dropped as new light filled in from behind.

Cicero turned to see two brawny, tough-looking men walking toward him. With the flicker of fire flowing over their faces, Cicero could not make out the men until they had closed in on him, but in that moment he recognized them as the Gauls from the procession crowd. They moved forward without a word.

"I am a consul of Rome. Understand what you are doing, men," Cicero said, his hands shaking.

The Gauls said nothing.

"Stop. You must STOP!" Cicero yelled to the men, but the Gauls did not listen. As they closed in farther, each raised an arm, readying the sword in their grasp to strike down Cicero.

From the side, a blade swung down from the darkness, cutting into the larger Gaul's arm, taking it from his body below the elbow. The Gaul cried out, falling to the ground as his companion turned just in time to deflect the next in-coming sword strike.

Cicero ducked, trying to stay out of the melee, as the sword strike came on with greater urgency. The larger Gaul, cradling his hemorrhaging stump and stumbling to his feet, darted away, leaving a flow of crimson in his wake. Seeing his companion flee, the smaller Gaul looked at Cicero a moment, then turned tail himself.

Cicero looked up to find Caesar's imposing bodyguard, Magnus, peering down with no more emotion than he had shown at the inauguration. Magnus reached down and grabbed Cicero by the shoulder and pulled him to his feet.

"Thank you, sir. Magnus, it is, right?" Cicero said through adrenaline-provoked chattering teeth. Magnus nodded and bent down to grab a satchel the smaller Gaul had dropped and the sword the larger Gaul had lost in the fighting—along with the arm still holding it. Magnus looked over the sword. Nodding approval of the cutlass, Magnus shoved off the severed limb's grip and tucked the sword into his belt. As the limb flopped to the ground with a haunting thud, Magnus nodded at Cicero to follow and head off down the alleyway.

"Yes. Let's go," Cicero said, following close behind his protector.

~

Cicero sipped wine as Caesar looked at the Gaul's sword that Magnus had brought back. "It's a Gallic blade, that much is certain," Caesar said, holding the sword by the hilt and swinging it with admiration of its craft.

"They definitely looked Gallic to me," Cicero said, taking another sip.

"So, you got a look at them during the fight? Magnus said he couldn't make out their features in the firelight," Caesar said.

"Well, first, I didn't know Magnus could talk, but more to the point, it was not during the fighting that I got my look at them. I saw them today at the end of the parade," Cicero said.

"You did?" Caesar said. "Two men? Definitely Gauls? Once larger than the other?"

"Yeah, that's them," Cicero said, astonished.

"I saw them too," Caesar said. "Catiline spoke with them before he left the inauguration today."

"No. That cannot be. You're talking coup. Even he wouldn't try something like that," Cicero said.

Caesar considered a moment, then grabbed the satchel, upturning it to expel its contents onto the table before them. As Caesar rifled through the items, Cicero plucked a letter out and read it.

"Wait, wait," Cicero said, handing the letter to Caesar.

"What is it?" Caesar asked.

"An armistice. It seems Catiline seeks to make peace with Gaul as a means for taking control of Rome," Cicero said.

"He must have others in the Senate with him on this," Caesar said.

"But who?" Cicero asked.

"Except for Lentulus and the obvious ones, I'm not certain," Caesar said. "That could be it, or it could be more. What do we do?"

Cicero sat back, thinking.

"However many it is, it will be near impossible to prove the guilt of anyone outside of Catiline himself," Cicero said. "But maybe it doesn't matter who's on his side. Much of Catiline's support comes from people whose debts he has bought up. They're only with him because of the power he wields over them. If we want to get Catiline, we need to take away that support."

"And how do we do that?" Caesar asked.

Cicero shrugged, "I'll present my argument."

Chapter Eighteen

Cicero sat at the head of the Senate, flipping through the pages he had written the night before. As tired as he had been yesterday, the attempt on his life had been more than up to the task of keeping Cicero up the entire night. Without respite, Cicero put quill to paper and wrote out his entire argument against Catiline from start to finish. When he finished, he rolled it up and made his way straight to the Curia. There was not a moment to spare.

As senators filed in, taking their seats and filling the room, Cicero thought of his children. To ensure their safety, he had sent them off to Terentia's family county estate well outside the city. At first, Terentia was defiant and uncompromising, still angry with Cicero from the years of their turbulent marriage, but when she finally saw the concern on his face, she did not question his instructions even though he was not able to explain the reason for them.

With the children gone and safe, Cicero was able to work unimpeded through the night. Exhausted though he was, the requirements of this most impactful of orations was enough to keep him going. Despite being prepared, Cicero was still a bundle of nerves. Not only had his life nearly been taken but an attempt had been made on the republic itself.

Certainly, Rome had seen its share of political conspiracies, and men like Marius and Sulla had forced their way into authoritarian control, but to attempt to kill one's political rival with the help of a foreign power was beyond the pale. If Catiline had been successful, it would have undermined the entire system and turned the cracks in the republic into ruinous fissures. Perhaps it was that weight that had caused Cicero such angst and had made his hands shake.

Cicero again looked over his words, trying to focus on the page and forget the rest of the world. He turned the page, his hand rattling the papyrus—

"Are you sure you're ready for this?" Caesar asked, seeing Cicero's shaking hands as he approached from behind.

"Ready doesn't matter when one has no choice in the matter. It has to be me giving this speech. And it has to be now. We cannot delay in the face of a coup," Cicero said.

"Well, it may not matter," Caesar said, looking around the room. "It's looking like he isn't showing up."

"He'll be here," Cicero said.

"How do you know?" Caesar asked.

"Because not showing up is admitting his guilt," Cicero said. "Catiline is a lot of things, but he is not one to admit to anything."

The chamber doors closed and Cicero and Caesar looked up to see Catiline and his entourage enter and make way to their side of the chamber. As Catiline sat, he made eye contact with Cicero. Catiline nodded cordially as if nothing had transpired. Any doubts Cicero might have had about Catiline's guilt now dissipated because of Catiline's nonchalant salutation.

"Good luck," Caesar said, patting Cicero on the shoulder as he headed out to take his seat.

The magistrate stepped to the fore and called out to the chamber, "I call to order this meeting of the Senate, Consul Marcus Tullia Cicero presiding."

Cicero took a calming breath. As his shaking hands finally stilled, Cicero stood, surprising the magistrate.

"Thank you, Magistrate," Cicero said. "I would like to break with custom and address the chamber straight away."

"Very well. It is within the bylaws to do so," the magistrate said, stepping away.

Catiline shifted uncomfortably as Cicero walked to the front of the landing. Cicero looked out across the congregation, scanning over each man. His gaze stopped on Catiline for a moment.

"When, oh, Catiline, do you mean to cease abusing our patience?" Cicero said directly to Catiline, but also addressing the room.

Catiline stiffened nervously.

"How long is that madness of yours still to mock us?" Cicero said. "When is there to be an end to your unbridled audacity, swaggering about as it does now?" Cicero paused, focusing his gaze on Catiline.

After a moment, Catiline started to rise, but from behind a hand pressed down on his shoulder, keeping him in his seat. He turned to find Caesar shaking his head. Catiline relented and sat back.

"Do not the guards on the Palatine Hill—do not the watches posted throughout the city—does not the alarm of the people, and the union of all good men—does not the precaution taken of the Senate in this most defensible place—do not the looks and countenances of this venerable body here present have any effect upon you?" Cicero said, captivating every soul in the room.

Catiline and Lentulus traded concerned looks.

"Do you not feel that your plans have been exposed?" Cicero continued. "Do you not see that your conspiracy has already been rendered powerless by the knowledge that everyone here now possesses of it?"

Catiline stood. "Do you have an accusation, sir, or must we all sit and endure you bloviating?" he cried out to the room.

"Yes, sir, I have an accusation. I accuse us all of betraying the republic," Cicero said to gasps in the chamber. "Shame on this time and on its principles for allowing your continued attacks against our holy republic. The Senate is aware of your dealings now; I, the consul, have seen the damning evidence of them; and yet you, Catiline, still live. You take a part in the public deliberations, as you watch and mark down and check off the planned slaughter of every one of us. And we, gallant men that we are, think that we are doing our duty to the republic if we keep out of the way of your frenzied attacks. Well, I will do so no more."

Cicero paused, looking out to the senators filling the room around him.

"Last night, that man tried to have me killed," Cicero said, pointing a finger in Catiline's direction, as the chamber burst into a murmur.

"Quiet!" the magistrate said, hammering his staff against the floor, silencing the room. "The consul has the floor. None other."

"This is outrageous," Catiline bellowed but paused as one of his cohorts stood and walked from Catiline to the other side of the chamber.

"I will have quiet!" the magistrate yelled again.

"But the man makes accusations and he does so without proof," Catiline said with feigned incredulity.

"Silence, I say—" the magistrate barked.

"It's fine, Magistrate. We should not expect Catiline to follow the rules of the Senate, since he refuses to follow the laws of the republic," Cicero said to laughs from the gallery. "But he has been accused and he deserves to see the evidence." Cicero turned from the magistrate and to the crowd. "But I am not here to accuse him of conspiring to kill the consul of Rome, I am here to accuse him of conspiring to kill the republic itself."

The crowd murmured loudly, which the magistrate silenced again with just two taps of his staff on the ground.

Two more of Catiline's cohorts stood and took seats on the other side of the room. Catiline's concern grew.

"You ought, Catiline, long ago to have been led to execution by command of the consul," Cicero said. "The destruction that you have been long plotting against us ought to have already fallen on your own head. But you have worked the system and leveraged your wealth to survive and thrive. No more."

Cicero waved a letter over his head. Catiline and Lentulus traded looks, as another handful of Catiline supporters retreated across the aisle.

"Please, listen while I speak of last night," Cicero said. "Last night, this document came to me and from it, you shall now see the outline for the destruction of the republic."

More of Catiline's people stood, leaving his side.

"On the very night of my inauguration," Cicero said, "as I walked to my home where my children live with me, I was met by the men who carried this document. But they did not greet me with salutations and well-wishes." Cicero looked to Catiline. "No, Catiline, your friends brought with them swords and threats."

Two more men exited Catiline's group, leaving just a handful of supporters.

"And I should have perished at the hands of accomplices in the same insanity and wickedness you've inflicted upon so many before me, if not for the foresight of a good friend and the protection of his man," Cicero said, nodding to Caesar and Magnus. Caesar nodded back; Magnus looked on unmoving.

"Do you dare to deny it, Catiline?" Cicero continued. "Why are you silent? I will prove it if you do deny it, for I also see here in the Senate some men who doubtless knew of your plans."

The remainder of Catiline's entourage, save for Lentulus, stepped away, sitting with the other sentators across the aisle.

"But I am not here to bemoan the attack on my life but that which you made against the republic. That is the crime for which there is no forgiveness," Cicero said. "And that is the crime that this document, this armistice makes clear."

Cicero held the document high, waving it to the crowd.

"Not content to accept the results of the election, our colleague and his companions conspired with our enemies, the Gauls, to band together and overthrow our government. Of which my death was to be only the beginning of a process of treason meant to seat Catiline as king of Rome."

The chamber gasped and chattered so loudly that the magistrate's staff seemed to make no sound as it met the ground in increasingly violent stomps. Through the madness, Lentulus stood and left Catiline's side.

As the chamber grew more silent, Catiline sat alone on his side of the aisle, the loneliest man in Rome.

Cicero stepped down, walking between the aisles and looking directly at Catiline. As he reached the middle of the room, Cicero faced Catiline with the entirety of the Senate behind him.

"With these omens, Catiline, be gone to your impious and nefarious war, to the great safety of the republic, to your own misfortune and injury, and to the destruction of those who have joined themselves to you in every wickedness and atrocity," Cicero said. "May you and your companions be repelled from your altars and from the temples—from the houses and walls of the city—from the lives and fortunes of all the citizens; and may this standard overwhelm all the enemies of good men, the foes of the republic, the robbers of Italy, men bound together by a treaty and infamous alliance of crimes, dead and alive and yoke them with eternal punishments."

Cicero stared at Catiline a moment, then turned, leaving Catiline alone, wilting under the gaze of every angry eye in the Senate.

Chapter Nineteen

"He must be put to death," Caesar said, slamming a fist on the table.

Cicero paced through his study. With two untouched plates of food on the table before them and the sun setting outside, Cicero and Caesar exhibited the ruffled hair and creased robes of two men who had spent an entire day in sustained discussions.

Caesar ran a hand through his hair and took a calming breath before looking again at Cicero. "They must all be put to death, Cicero," Caesar said. "There is no other course to take."

"And they will be after I prosecute them for their crimes," Cicero said.

Since Cicero's masterful oration against Catiline before the Senate, some of Catiline's conspirators had been uncovered, many from the Senate itself. Lentulus Sura was the least surprising of the group, though he too had turned against Catiline by the end of Cicero's speech. Indeed, all of Catiline's fellow conspirators within the Senate had turned on him to save their own skins, which said something about Catiline and the company he kept. In total, Cicero was able to implicate five others, including Lentulus, in Catiline's plot, but he was certain there were many more.

"You can't go to trial with Catiline," Caesar said.

"I have to," Cicero said. "I can't let him go free, not after what he did. And I can't send him to his death without a trial. It goes against all the laws of the republic."

"Yes, but he also went against the laws of the republic," Caesar said, taking a sip of wine and finally paying some attention to the food that had been sitting before them for the better part of the day.

"You're right, Caesar. Of course, you're right, but it has to be proven in court. Otherwise, who are we to punish him for going against the laws of the republic if we do not follow them ourselves?" Cicero asked.

Caesar considered a moment, spitting an olive pit into his fist and depositing it into a bowl. "Under normal circumstances," Caesar said, "you are correct, but these circumstances are not normal. He did not go just against the laws of the republic, he went against the Republic itself."

Cicero started to speak, but Caesar waved him off.

"Hold on a moment," Caesar said, collecting his thoughts. "Let's assume you're able to prosecute and defeat Catiline. What of the others? Yes, they are implicated by circumstance, but there is little else to hang a conviction on. Nothing short of Catiline giving them all up will find them on the losing side of a trial, so they'll all still be out there to continue to undermine you."

Cicero considered Caesar's words.

"There has to be a better answer," Cicero said. "If I put Catiline to death without a trial, I'm breaking the laws of the republic. I'll be a political pariah."

"I apologize if my counsel is lacking, but I see only two options and just one of them is the right one," Caesar said.

Cicero finally sat down and picked at the plate of food before him, letting his mind wander. He had worked his entire life to reach the consulship, and now his time was dedicated not to his job, but to punishing the man he beat out for it. Cicero should have been working on republic business and devising reforms to keep the system intact. Yet, despite his victory Cicero's thoughts were not of the republic but of Catiline. Perhaps Caesar was right. Perhaps the only way to save the republic was to break its rules, but Cicero still could not accept such a thought.

"There is a man whose opinion you have not yet sought and he has more experience in such matters than the entirety of the Senate," Caesar said.

"Who?" Cicero asked.

"Sulla," Caesar said.

Cicero nodded. Sulla either controlled the republic or was maneuvering through it for years. Caesar was right; nobody had dealt with more ambiguous and politically dangerous situations within the republic than he had.

"Of course, you're right," Cicero said. "But does it not seem contradictory to our aims to seek advice on deciding Catiline's fate from the man who was Catiline's role model?"

"Perhaps, but is good counsel not good counsel regardless of the mouth from which it comes?" Caesar said.

"Yes, you're right. Of course, that is the wise decision. Listening to the man's thoughts would be wise, and it does not require acting on them," Cicero said.

Caesar nodded and went back to picking at the wedge of bread on his plate. Cicero watched Caesar fumble with his food, as his face contorted into a frown.

"Something vexes you, my friend," Cicero asked.

"What? No," Caesar said. "I just…" Caesar paused looking outside into the dying light of the day.

"What?" Cicero asked, concerned by his friend's preoccupation.

Caesar contemplated a moment longer, then turned to Cicero. "I'm concerned that you do not understand the weight of the situation you find yourself in," Caesar said.

"I *do* understand. Of course I do. I am in danger and I know it, but I am not swapping my ethics for my safety when the very future of the republic depends on my deft handling of the situation," Cicero said.

"But maybe the republic *is* the problem, Cicero," Caesar said. "You wrap yourself in the republic and indeed you are its greatest warrior, but Catiline is just a symptom of the problem. Everything we're toiling over is inconsequential because no matter what happens to Catiline and no matter how you choose to deal with him, the damage Marius and Sulla did cannot be reversed. We need to be looking out for ourselves now."

"So, what are you saying?" Cicero asked. "It isn't worth fighting to keep the republic alive anymore?"

"No, I'm saying that maybe there's nothing left to fight for," Caesar said. "Everything may appear intact, but its fate was decided long before we had a say.

"The republic is dead, Cicero."

Cicero left in the early morning, kissing his sleeping children before meeting with the caravan of guards that would take him through the countryside and into Puteoli. Riding horseback had always been a little too rough and tumble for Cicero's tastes, but he had no desire to walk the many miles ahead, and sitting in a litter while the other men towed him along didn't seem desirable either. So, here he was, saddled atop a black steed as the caravan marched along the countryside in the crisp January air.

Though he had not looked forward to the long day's ride, as Cicero peered out on the sprawling countryside and took in the fresh air, he relaxed for the first time in weeks. If for just that moment, Cicero's mind wandered from his Catiline conundrum.

Sulla's aging, arthritic hands penetrated the rich soil churning up and down, tilling the clumps of earth loose. Parting the dirt, he patted down the edges to form an indentation and looked back toward his pre-teen grandson hovering nearby.

"The seeds, my boy," Sulla said, as his grandson riffled through a leather pouch, finally handing over a trickle of seeds.

"Now, we drop three in, then cover them," Sulla said, going through the actions as he spoke of them. "Give it a little pat, so the wind doesn't blow the dirt and seeds away, then give it some water."

The boy nodded, struggling to lift a heavy bucket as he poured a drizzle of water from it.

Hearing a horse, Sulla looked up to see a caravan approach. He looked back to his grandson. "You sow the rest of the seeds on your own. Understand?" he said as he stood, grunting from the strain on his declining body. He smacked his hands together rhythmically, ridding them of soil as he walked toward the road.

Easing along through the rows of cabbage growing in front of his vast estate, Sulla approached the caravan. He smiled as a familiar face rode up before him.

"I had been expecting this visit earlier," Sulla said to Cicero. "Come inside and let's talk."

~

Cicero looked at Sulla's trembling hand as it poured wine from the pitcher it wielded. The thin skin and bulbous, painfully swollen joints jolted Cicero with the realization of Sulla's much-advanced age.

"That noticeable, huh?" Sulla said, setting the wine pitcher aside.

"No, sir, I just—"

"Don't start lying to me now, Cicero!" Sulla said with a smirk.

"I'm sorry, sir. I guess it's just been a while since I last saw you," Cicero said.

"Yes, and age seems to speed its process the more of it one attains," Sulla said looking on his hands. "The changes are gradual and I live with them every day, so I don't notice, but I see it in the eyes of those who do."

"Are you well, sir?" Cicero asked.

"Ah, I'm fine. Just a bout of mortality," Sulla said. "But let's not dwell on the inevitability of my situation. Let's talk about your decision."

Cicero sat upright and alert, surprised.

"Don't be so shocked," Sulla said. "I still have my men in Rome. I still get reports on the happenings. And it sounds as though you're struggling with a big happening right now."

"Catiline," Cicero said, hating even the sound of the name.

"You want to know what it is you should do with him," Sulla said. "Well, there's only one thing you can do. He made an attempt on your life. You need—you *must* take his."

"Yes, sir," Cicero said, "but a consul of Rome cannot just kill a man."

"Of course you can, you just don't want to deal with the ramifications," Sulla said.

"It would undermine the system to execute these men without a trial," Cicero said.

"Or is it that it would undermine *you*?" Sulla asked.

"How can a consul be trusted if he does not apply the same laws to himself as he does on others?" Cicero asked.

"It's a contradiction for certain. But you can't risk putting him on trial, can you?" Sulla asked.

"No. It gives him a platform for his lies. And if he isn't convicted, then he's free to further his plot against the republic," Cicero said.

"He's a danger to your credibility if you kill him, but a danger to the republic if you don't," Sulla said.

"So what's the right answer?" Cicero asked.

"There is no right answer," Sulla said.

Cicero sighed, rubbing his brow in annoyance.

"I'm not trying to be obtuse, Cicero," Sulla said.

"Then what is your counsel, sir?" Cicero said.

"Exactly as I just said. There is no right answer," Sulla said, as Cicero slumped. "That's the reality of the big job. You have your ideas and your plans going into it, but when you're actually sitting there in the big chair and the problems pile up in front of you, it's never cut and dry. Most often you have pressure from all over to make a choice, but all you have to choose from are wrong answers."

Cicero sighed.

"Not the answer you were looking for, is it?" Sulla said.

"No," Cicero said. "But maybe it is what I needed to hear."

"Well, I suspect you already know what you have to do," Sulla said. "Now, you just have to do it."

Cicero nodded and stood, putting his hand out to his former mentor. "Thank you for your time, sir," Cicero said.

"Nonsense. Thank *you* for caring about the ruminations of an old man," Sulla said.

Cicero nodded and turned to leave.

"Cicero…" Sulla said, as Cicero looked back to him. "I fear you were right."

"Right? About what, sir?" Cicero asked.

"I opened the door for tyrants and now there's no way to close it again," Sulla said.

"Perhaps, sir," Cicero said. "But I'll do everything I can to fight that."

The clatter of a full house of senators bled into the back room as Cicero looked over the notes of a speech. On the journey home he'd had much time to think about Sulla's words, but in the end, just as Sulla had said, Cicero already knew the choice he had to make.

Caesar stepped into the chambers. Seeing Cicero, he hurried to him.

"You're back," Caesar said. "What of Sulla's advice?"

"It wasn't so much advice, as it was him telling me what I needed to hear," Cicero said. "And that reminded me that my duty is to the republic, not myself."

"And what does that mean?" Caesar asked.

"It means that even if I have to betray my own honor, I have to do what is best for the republic," Cicero said. "Catiline and his conspirators must be put to death."

Caesar looked back, considering.

"You were right," Cicero said, wondering why Caesar was not more accepting of the solution. "It'll undermine my consulship and my reputation, but it's the only way to protect the republic. Catiline's death will end his plotting and serve as a new standard for punishment for all who conspire against the republic. I'm sorry I didn't listen to you before, but you were right."

"But what if there is another way?" Caesar asked.

"If you know one, don't bother with preamble," Cicero said, setting aside his speech.

Caesar gathered his thoughts for a moment.

"I've spoken with Pompey and Crassus. They share our concerns about Catiline and the republic, and they wish to form an alliance," Caesar said.

"That's ideal. Those are august men and we could certainly build a coalition in the Senate with them, but how does it help with the Catiline situation?" Cicero asked.

"They want you to exile him," Caesar said.

"Wait. You were the one insisting that he has to die," Cicero said.

"And I believed that, but if you put Catiline to death, your power as consul will be gone," Caesar said. "You'll never recover politically. But Pompey and Crassus are the richest men in Rome. If you exile Catiline and retain your clout, we can combine it with their wealth and the strength of my legions and we can control Rome."

"Control Rome?" Cicero asked. "The Senate controls Rome."

"The Senate is corrupt and inept," Caesar said. "Rome needs powerful leadership to get things done now."

Cicero stared back at Caesar, studying his face. Cicero had known Caesar long enough to recognize when he was being sincere. Cicero's stomach sank.

"I'm sorry, my friend, but I have a speech to give," Cicero said.

"It's madness to follow that path, Cicero," Caesar said. "Come with us. Just exile Catiline and his fellow conspirators. After some time, they can mysteriously disappear, but you'll retain your political clout. Think of everything you can do for the republic with the trust the people and the Senate have in you."

"But what is that trust worth, if one is not trustworthy?" Cicero asked. "What you're proposing sounds like sedition, Caesar."

Caesar sighed and shook his head.

"The republic is sinking, Cicero," Caesar said. "It's been battered against the rocks and now it's taking on water. I can see land. Come with me to it."

Cicero looked sadly at Caesar.

"I'm sorry, my friend," Cicero said. "You're right. I know you are right. The republic is sinking and all good sense and instincts for self-preservation scream to abandon it, but it's not myself that I'm trying to preserve. I will stay at my post and bail water from its haul until we are both taken from this Earth."

Cicero looked at Caesar a moment, then stepped away.

Cicero entered the chamber and went to his seat at the head of the room but remained standing. The magistrate stepped to the fore, silencing the room with two knocks of his staff against the marble floor.

"I call the Senate to order," the magistrate announced. "The discussions of the day shall start with—"

"I wish to address the chamber before we begin our business," Cicero said, stepping beside the magistrate.

"Very well. Honorable Consul Cicero has the floor," the magistrate said.

The words sank into Cicero, making him sick to his stomach. His entire life had led to him reaching this position and now he was going to sully it all by acting against the laws of the republic and demand the execution of the conspirators without a trial. But he could not let any such ambivalence show. Today, he had to feign confidence, because even if his actions destroyed his reputation, they would also protect the republic.

"Citizens of the republic," Cicero said, "Today I stand before you to not call for—"

Cicero paused, as Caesar stood. Slipping out from the stepped seats and to the floor of the chamber, Caesar moved toward Cicero. Clomp…clomp…clomp… Caesar's sandal-covered footfalls echoed through the otherwise silent chamber. As he approached Cicero, Caesar held out to him a small piece of parchment. Cicero took the note and the old friends looked at each other mournfully. After a moment, Caesar broke away and made his way to the exit.

Cicero watched his friend walk out, waiting until Caesar exited before unfolding the parchment.

Cicero—

I must swim for shore now. Do try to keep your head above water.
Your friend,
Gaius Julius Caesar

Cicero stared at the note for a moment, then folded it, tucking it away into a pocket. He took a breath and looked around the room at the many august men surrounding him. Cicero realized these were the last moments before his duty washed away his ambitions. He took a breath and looked at his hands. Fighting off their slight tremble, he made fists.

"Citizens, what I demand of you today, I do only for the republic…"

Chapter Twenty

Cicero's quill glided across the parchment, working without recess, as his workers sped through the villa, rushing to pack the goods he'd spent a lifetime curating. Nervous chatter and rushed footsteps filled the air with noise, but Cicero remained focused on the parchment before him. Seated outside at a desk overlooking the entirety of Rome, even that view did not deter Cicero from his task. Coming to the end, Cicero paused to look it over, then flipped back to the front of the manuscript. On the cover he wrote: "On Duty."

Running his hand over the scroll, Cicero paused, looking on the vellum-thin skin of his aging hands. His mind wandered to that day so long ago when he had noticed the same age-worn skin on Sulla's hands. Sulla died within months of Cicero's visit, so they never saw each other again. Cicero looked out on the city and his mind wandered to the past.

Following his final oration against Catiline and his conspirators, the political melee engulfed Cicero in controversy. Despite the politically ruinous headwinds, Cicero absorbed the objections and stayed true to his mission. On December 5, 63 BC, Cicero's orders to execute the conspirators were enacted and a precedent for future threats to the republic was created. Cicero personally walked Lentulus to Tullianum Prison to oversee his execution.

As fate had it, Catiline managed to use his connections to get out of the city and avoid execution. But Catiline could not avert his fate forever, finding his end on the battlefield when his fraying insurgent army broke ranks and abandoned him midfight.

Cicero served his entire term as consul but never recovered from the controversy. His Catiline Orations became the stuff of legend, serving as the model for his rhetorical style, but he became a political pariah nonetheless. And as Caesar officially formed his triumvirate with Crassus and Pompey, Cicero again found himself in exile from Rome.

For over a year, Cicero lived in Northern Greece, exiled not just from Rome but from his children too. He fell into a depression. Rudderless without his career, Cicero finally dug himself out of his melancholia when he was recalled to Rome where he again worked to solidify himself as the republic's most ardent defender.

Politically, Cicero never completely recovered from his lawless execution of the Catiline conspirators, but in time he regained his footing and became relevant again. More importantly, Cicero's actions against the attempted usurpers managed to stabilize the republic—but only for a while.

Once Cicero returned from exile, Caesar's triumvirate loomed large, but it was not until the triumvirate dissolved that the true danger to the republic became clear, as Caesar used his military might to take Rome and install himself as dictator. Cicero worked with Caesar in hopes that he might restore the republic, but after Caesar was assassinated, chaos reigned when Caesar's second, Mark Antony, created a second triumvirate with Caesar's nephew and adopted son, Octavian, and the wealthy noble Marcus Lepidus.

Thinking Antony a mindless, self-aggrandizing thug, Cicero worked with Octavian, trying to help the young man develop into a great leader. Indeed, Cicero's lessons guided and enlightened the young Octavian, but when Antony added Cicero to the proscribed kill list, Octavian was left in a difficult spot. Octavian fought Antony for days, trying to save Cicero's life and keep him off the list. In the end, Antony got his way, and early one morning Cicero received word from an insider that he was to be killed.

Despite the warnings of his imminent death, Cicero remained calm enough to finish work on his scroll. But now that the scroll was completed and Cicero looked out over Rome, emotion took hold of him. It was not fear that he felt but the wistful pang of nostalgia that old memories had a way of stirring. Looking out on his home of all those years, Cicero saw nothing but memories of a life fully realized.

"Father, what are you doing?" Tullia said, stepping out into the courtyard with Cicero's granddaughter in her arms. "We must leave."

"I'm just enjoying the view," Cicero said.

Tullia approached, concerned.

"Are you not well, Father?" Tullia asked with an examining eye.

"Of course, my dear," Cicero said, motioning out at the city. "Isn't it beautiful? I fear I have not properly indulged my senses in the beauty around us."

Marcus Minor stepped out, incredulous to find his father and sister seemingly engaged in a relaxed conversation.

"What are you waiting for?" Marcus said. "We must leave. Now."

Cicero nodded; calmly, he picked up his scroll and stood up.

As Marcus, Tullia, and the servants worked feverishly to load the wagons with the goods from the house, Cicero held his baby granddaughter, motioning playfully at her with his fingers.

"That's it," Tullia said. "That's everything. Let's go."

"All of my scrolls are on there?" Cicero asked.

"Yes, Father. Everything you've written and as many of your collection as I could fit," Marcus said.

"Perfect," Cicero said, handing over the baby to Marcus. "And make sure this one makes it too." Cicero handed Tullia the scroll he just finished.

"Why don't you just hold on to it?" Tullia asked.

"Because I'm not going with you, my dear," Cicero said.

"What? No," Marcus said. "Just get on the wagon."

"No, son, I'm staying. Antony only proscribed me, so you'll be fine, but please make certain my works are safe," Cicero said.

"Father, no. You can't stay. They'll kill you," Tullia said.

"Perhaps, but I'm not leaving the city in exile again," Cicero said. "I've done that enough already.

"The republic is falling, Father," Marcus said.

"Then I shall fall with it," Cicero said, kissing both children, then his granddaughter. "I love you both, but this is my wish. Please respect it."

Tullia and Marcus slumped, but, seeing their father's quiet resolve, they relented. Marcus helped Tullia and the child onto a wagon and guided the yoked oxen along. Cicero looked on as they disappeared down the road.

Stepping back into his courtyard, Cicero sat and looked out on the city, as the sun waned in the sky. Time passed unnoticed, as he simply existed in the moment with his dying republic. Even as the pounding against his villa doors began, his steady gaze did not waver. Even as the doors crashed open, giving way to a clatter of marching steps, Cicero did not stir. Not until the soldiers surrounded him did he acknowledge the men who had come to take his life.

"A lovely view, wouldn't you say?" Cicero said to the legionaries.

The soldiers traded looks, not used to such serenity in a man in Cicero's position.

"Sir, you have been placed on the proscribed list," the lead soldier said.

Cicero looked back out at Rome and took in a deep, measured breath. He looked to the lead soldier.

"There's nothing proper in what you're doing, soldier, but do try to kill me properly," Cicero said leaning forward, exposing his neck for the soldier's blade.

As the shadow of the soldier's rising blade passed along the soil beneath him, Cicero looked to his hands. They did not shake.

About the Author

Eric D. Martin is a novelist and screenwriter. He has a B.A. in Film Studies from the University of California, Santa Barbara, and an M.F.A. in Screen and Television Writing from Pepperdine University. While studying at Pepperdine, Eric served as president of the student film society, Courier 12, and was a semifinalist for the Academy of Arts and Sciences Nicholl Fellowship. Recently, Eric adapted the novel *The Liar's Chair* for the screen and wrote the popular Lifetime thriller, *The Other Mother*. Currently, Eric is writing for the premium cable television drama *Heels*, for Starz, and developing the TV comedy *King Elizabeth*.

NOW AVAILABLE FROM THE MENTORIS PROJECT

America's Forgotten Founding Father
A Novel Based on the Life of Filippo Mazzei
by Rosanne Welch

A. P. Giannini—The People's Banker
by Francesca Valente

Christopher Columbus: His Life and Discoveries
by Mario Di Giovanni

Fermi's Gifts
A Novel Based on the Life of Enrico Fermi
by Kate Fuglei

God's Messenger
The Astounding Achievements of Mother Cabrini
A Novel Based on the Life of Mother Frances X. Cabrini
by Nicole Gregory

Harvesting the American Dream
A Novel Based on the Life of Ernest Gallo
by Karen Richardson

Marconi and His Muses
A Novel Based on the Life of Guglielmo Marconi
by Pamela Winfrey

Soldier, Diplomat, Archaeologist
A Novel Based on the Bold Life of Louis Palma di Cesnola
by Peg A. Lamphier

COMING SOON FROM THE MENTORIS PROJECT

A Novel Based on the Life of Alessandro Volta
A Novel Based on the Life of Amerigo Vespucci
A Novel Based on the Life of Andrea Palladio
A Novel Based on the Life of Angelo Dundee
A Novel Based on the Life of Antonin Scalia
A Novel Based on the Life of Antonio Meucci
A Novel Based on the Life of Buzzie Bavasi
A Novel Based on the Life of Cesare Becaria
A Novel Based on the Life of Federico Fellini
A Novel Based on the Life of Filippo Brunelleschi
A Novel Based on the Life of Frank Capra
A Novel Based on the Life of Galileo Galilei
A Novel Based on the Life of Giovanni Andrea Doria
A Novel Based on the Life of Giovanni di Bicci de' Medici
A Novel Based on the Life of Giuseppe Garibaldi
A Novel Based on the Life of Giuseppe Verdi
A Novel Based on the Life of Guido Monaco
A Novel Based on the Life of Harry Warren
A Novel Based on the Life of Henry Mancini
A Novel Based on the Life of John Cabot
A Novel Based on the Life of Judge John Sirica
A Novel Based on the Life of Lenonardo Covello
A Novel Based on the Life of Leonardo de Vinci
A Novel Based on the Life of Luca Pacioli
A Novel Based on the Life of Maria Montessori
A Novel Based on the Life of Mario Andretti
A Novel Based on the Life of Mario Cuomo
A Novel Based on the Life of Niccolo Machiavelli
A Novel Based on the Life of Peter Rodino
A Novel Based on the Life of Pietro Belluschi
A Novel Based on the Life of Publius Cornelius Scipio
A Novel Based on the Life of Robert Barbera
A Novel Based on the Life of Saint Augustine of Hippo
A Novel Based on the Life of Saint Francis of Assisi
A Novel Based on the Life of Saint Thomas Aquinas
A Novel Based on the Life of Vince Lombardi

For more information on these titles and
The Mentoris Project, please visit
www.mentorisproject.org.